THE BOBBSEY TWINS
AT MYSTERY MANSION

"Did you lose the key, Freddie?" Nan asked.

The Bobbsey Twins
At Mystery Mansion

By

LAURA LEE HOPE

GROSSET & DUNLAP

Publishers   New York

Printed in the United States of America

Linda Alexander

CONTENTS

CONTENTS

THE BOBBSEY TWINS
AT MYSTERY MANSION

CHAPTER I

WAGGO'S FIND

"Sit up, Waggo!" Freddie Bobbsey called out.

The little fox terrier obeyed immediately. He sat up on his hind legs and held out his front paws toward his young master. Freddie was not the little dog's only master. Waggo belonged to the whole Bobbsey family, but right now Freddie was in charge of him. The boy was putting on a show on the front lawn of his home. Several children had gathered to watch the dog do his tricks.

"Now ask for your supper," said Freddie.

Waggo gave several short barks, and Freddie threw him a puppy biscuit.

At this moment his twin sister Flossie, blue-eyed and curly-haired, came from the house. She looked very much like Freddie, and liked to play with him, even though he often got the two of them into trouble.

"Hello, Flossie," called a little girl from the group of children on the lawn.

"Hello, Joan," Flossie replied. "Hello, everybody!"

"I wish I had a dog like Waggo," said Joan Johnson. Her own pet had gone away two years before.

"Maybe your dog Sport will come back some day," said Flossie kindly.

"I don't think so," replied Joan. "He's been gone too long."

"Did he go away by himself?" asked Freddie.

Joan said her mother and father thought the dog had been stolen. They were sure, though, that if he could have got loose he would have come home.

"I guess I'll never see him again," sighed Joan. "Freddie, make Waggo do some more tricks."

But Waggo did not want to show off any longer. He had finished eating the puppy biscuit and now ran down the street. One by one the children wandered off. Freddie and Flossie were about to go into the house when they saw their brother and sister, who were a few years older, coming up the street with several bundles. The small twins decided to wait and see what might be in the packages.

The older children were twins also. Their names were Bert and Nan Bobbsey. They had dark hair and eyes, and looked alike, but they did not look at all like Freddie and Flossie.

"Let me open the packages!" cried Flossie, as Bert and Nan reached the front walk.

"You'd better ask Mother first," said Nan. "They're hers."

The younger twins might have been more insistent about looking into the packages, if something else had not happened at that moment. Bert, who had turned around to look down the street, uttered a cry of surprise.

"Just see what Waggo's bringing home," he said.

The other Bobbsey children looked at the little dog. In his mouth he was carrying a fuzzy, gray kitten by the back of its neck. The kitten was bent double, resembling a ball of fur, and its eyes were almost closed.

"Oh, the poor kitty," cried Flossie, as she saw it struggle to get away. "Waggo will kill it!"

Nan assured her little sister that Waggo was carrying the kitten in the proper fashion. Just the same, she too was a little worried that the dog might hurt it. She ran to meet Waggo and took the kitten from his mouth.

"Where in the world did you get this?" she asked him.

Waggo barked several times and wagged his tail very fast. This did not help Nan find out who the owner of the kitten might be. She asked the other children if they had noticed where Waggo had been, but none of them had.

"We'll just have to inquire at the different houses to find the owner," she decided.

Bert took the bundles into the hall, then the four children started off. They took turns ringing doorbells and asking, "Does this kitten belong to you?" Though they covered nearly five square blocks, no one claimed the little cat.

"We'll have to keep her," said Flossie quietly. She was carrying the kitten now, cuddling it against her cheek. The cat was purring contentedly, and Flossie was sure it would like to live at the Bobbsey home.

"Maybe Snap won't like to have a kitten around," said Bert.

Snap was the Bobbseys' older dog. He had been with them ever since the twins could remember. Snap had not liked it when young Waggo had come to live at the house, because Waggo was very active and mischievous. Snap wanted to sleep most of the time and did not like to be disturbed.

For this reason, when they entered the front door, the children went directly to Snap, who was lying in front of the living room fireplace.

"Here's a new little sister for you," said Flossie, holding the kitten near the old dog's head.

He sniffed inquiringly for a minute, then went back to sleep.

"I guess he doesn't mind," the little girl said. "I'm going to show Pussy to Mother."

She went upstairs for a few minutes, then returned, smiling happily. Mrs. Bobbsey had said they might keep the kitten! Next, the children went to introduce it to Dinah, who was their nice Negro cook. The elderly woman was busy kneading bread with her hands, and singing merrily. Someone had given the Bobbseys an up-to-date bread mixer, but Dinah had scorned this. She felt sure she could make better bread with her hands than any machine could.

"Lawsy me!" she exclaimed when she saw the kitten. "Where'd yo' all get dat?"

Nan explained that Waggo had picked it up, and that they had been unable to find its owner. Flossie added it was going to live with them.

"My goodness me," said Dinah. "Pretty soon you'll have a menagerie around dis place. Yo' got one ole cat already and two dogs."

The children were worried for a moment that the cook would object to having a kitten around. But she smiled broadly and said:

"De poor thing looks hungry. Yo' better get it a little dish o' milk."

While Flossie and Freddie went to do this, Nan tried to figure out where the new kitten might sleep. A pillow or a little box would do. She asked Bert what he thought.

"How about a basket?" he said. "Harper's store is having a sale of cat and dog baskets. We might get one."

"Oh, that would be the best thing," agreed Nan. "I'll ask Mother for the money."

Mrs. Bobbsey smiled at her daughter's enthusiasm. Pleased that her children always were kind to animals, she gladly got her purse. There were no one-dollar bills in it, so she handed Nan a five-dollar bill.

"Don't spend it all," she said, as the girl went out the door. "Two dollars should be enough."

The younger twins wanted to go downtown to help select the basket, but Dinah thought someone

ought to stay at home and take care of the kitten.
Freddie and Flossie said they would stay. The little
boy got a ball of cord from a drawer and rolled it
across the kitchen floor. At once the kitten ran after
it and daintily tapped it with one of her front paws.

"Now yo' all take yo' pet out o' my kitchen," said
Dinah. "I'se got to make some dessert fo' dinner and
I don't want to get dat new kitten in de pudding by
mistake," she laughed.

Flossie and Freddie carried the kitten into the living room, while Bert and Nan started for the business section of Lakeport.

Just as the older twins reached Main Street, Nan
saw an elderly woman whom she knew walking toward them. She had a paper box in her hand.

"Here comes Aunt Sallie Pry," she said to her
brother, who was looking in a store window.

The woman was not a real aunt to the Bobbsey
twins, but she had often taken care of them. They
liked her very much, but it was difficult sometimes to
make her understand things because she was deaf.

"Good morning, children," she said upon reaching them. "How are all your family?"

"Oh, everyone's fine," Nan replied in a loud voice.
"We have a new kitten, but she has no bed. Mother
said we might buy a basket."

"Try a biscuit?" said Aunt Sallie. "I'm sorry, but
there aren't any biscuits in this box."

"No, we don't want a biscuit. A basket," said
Nan. "We have a new kitten. We're going to buy a
bed for it to sleep in."

"A kitten?" repeated Mrs. Pry. "I often take my cat to bed with me too," she added.

Bert and Nan tried hard to keep from smiling at the mix-up.

Aunt Sallie told them she was waiting for a bus to carry her out to Sing Foo's mansion.

"What is that?" shouted Bert.

"Oh, haven't you heard?" the woman said. "On the outskirts of town lives a nice old Chinese. He has a big house with lovely gardens and flowers. I may go there to take care of them."

"You mean the flowers?" asked Nan.

"Oh, I hope it won't shower," said Aunt Sallie, looking at the sky. "I didn't bring my umbrella."

Nan spoke a little louder. "Are you going to take care of Sing Foo's gardens?"

"Oh, no," Mrs. Pry replied. "I'm just going to take care of his house."

The elderly woman asked Bert and Nan if they would like to go out with her sometime to see the place. She told them it had an interesting history, and, in fact, was rather mysterious. They begged her to tell them more, but she said there was no time now.

"Here comes my bus," she added, looking up the street. "I hope you enjoy your new kitten. But be careful about letting it get on the bed. You know they like to claw and make holes in things."

With this warning the elderly lady waved her hand and stepped into the street. Bert helped her get on the bus. Then the twins went on.

"What do you suppose Aunt Sallie meant by Sing Foo's house being mysterious?" Nan asked her brother.

"I wonder," he said. "I do hope she'll take us out there sometime."

In a few minutes the twins reached Harper's store. Because of the sale, the place was full of people. So many of them were buying small baskets that the children wondered if there would be one left for their new kitten. At last a clerk came to wait on them. She showed the twins what was left, and after looking over the baskets, Nan decided on a brown wicker one.

"Do you think this one will be all right, Bert?"

"Sure," he said. "I'll go over and pay for it. Where's the money?"

Nan handed him the five-dollar bill her mother had given her. As soon as the clerk had written out the check, Bert took it to a desk in the corner of the store.

"Here's the money for a basket we bought," he said to the man who stood there.

The Bobbsey boy began to figure out how much change he should receive, and decided that it would be three dollars and two cents. Looking up, he was surprised that the man evidently had not yet figured the amount, because he was still fingering the five-dollar bill. After turning it over several times, he handed it back to Bert.

"I'm sorry, son," he said, "but this money is no good."

"What do you mean?" the boy asked.

"I mean the bill is a counterfeit."

Bert stared first at the man, then at the bill. He could not believe what he had just heard. The man must have thought the boy did not understand because he said:

"Your bill is a counterfeit. That means it's no good. It's fake money."

"But my mother gave it to me," Bert protested.

"I can't help that. It's still no good. You'll have to give me a dollar and ninety-eight cents of good money if you want the basket."

Bert picked up the five-dollar bill. What was he going to do? He had no other money with him. As he turned from the desk he met Nan coming toward him.

"What's the matter?" she asked, noting a queer look on his face.

"Somebody gave Mother a bad five-dollar bill," Bert replied. "The man says it's not real money!"

CHAPTER II

THE FAKE MONEY

"OUR money is no good?" cried Nan.

"That's what the man said," Bert answered.

The twins had spoken more loudly than they realized. Several people in the store heard their remarks and came over to look at the counterfeit five-dollar bill in Bert's hand. Suddenly a boy pushed his way through the crowd. He gave an unpleasant laugh as if he were glad Bert Bobbsey was in trouble.

"So you tried to cheat Mr. Harper, did you?" he said loudly so that everybody could hear him. "Passing bad money, eh?"

Bert and Nan looked at the disagreeable boy. He was Danny Rugg, a lad whom they both disliked very much. They always had had difficulty with him.

Some time before Danny had accused Bert of being afraid of a ghost, and the two boys had fought over the remark. This was fully related in the story called "The Bobbsey Twins." In the children's most recent adventure, "The Bobbsey Twins on the Pony Trail," Danny had given Flossie and Freddie some pills to make them grow tall in a hurry, and had caused a lot of other trouble.

Danny Rugg was not very popular with the people in Lakepoit. Quite the opposite was true of the Bobbseys. Almost everyone knew them and liked them. Mr. Bobbsey was in the lumber business and was on the town council. Mrs. Bobbsey did a great deal of work for charity.

When the children's parents were not at home, kind and dependable Dinah took care of the twins. Dinah's husband Sam worked for Mr. Bobbsey at the lumber yard and did odd jobs around the house. Bert and Nan were old enough to help their father at the lumber yard and do some of the chores at home. They enjoyed helping their parents and prided themselves on being able to do things well.

Now, as Bert stood in Harper's store, he felt bad because he would not be able to buy the basket for the new kitten. Before he had a chance to reply to Danny Rugg, the bully said:

"So you thought you'd get away with something, did you? Well, I'm glad Mr. Harper caught you before you cheated him out of any money."

This was too much for Bert. Like lightning he doubled up his fists and started menacingly toward Danny. But Danny was prepared for a fight. He, too, doubled up his fists.

"What's going on here?" demanded a man's voice, and Mr. Harper himself pushed his way through the group of customers.

Danny saw him coming. Quickly he ducked beneath the arm of a woman and ran from the store.

The man behind the desk called out to Mr.

Harper and explained about Bert's five-dollar bill. The store owner took the money from the boy's hand and looked at it carefully.

"Yes, the cashier is right," he said. "It's too bad, Bert, but I'm afraid we cannot accept it. What was it you bought?"

"A basket. A basket for our kitten, sir."

Mr. Harper, who knew the Bobbsey family well, said it would be all right for Bert to charge the amount, and bring the money to him the next time he was downtown.

"How can you tell this five-dollar bill is no good?" Nan asked the man.

Before replying, Mr. Harper requested that the cashier hand him a good five-dollar bill. He held this next to the counterfeit.

"Do you see any difference?" he inquired, smiling at the twins.

Bert and Nan had to confess that they did not see any. Mr. Harper took a pencil from his pocket and pointed to the picture of Abraham Lincoln on the front of the bills. "Look carefully at the two heads," he said.

In a moment Nan cried out, "Oh, I see! On the good bill Mr. Lincoln has a lock of hair on his forehead, and the counterfeit hasn't any."

"That's right," said Mr. Harper. "And I'll show you another way to find out whether or not bills are good."

He carried the money over to a counter and tore off a piece of white wrapping paper. Crumpling up the good bill, he rubbed it against the wrapping paper. Several green marks appeared. He did the same thing with the fake money, but it did not make a single mark on the white sheet.

"Oh, isn't that clever!" cried Nan, and thanked Mr. Harper for having shown them how to tell the difference.

Other people in the store began to talk about the counterfeit money. Some of them wondered if they, too, might have some with them. Hurriedly women began looking through their purses and men pulled wallets from their pockets to examine the bills in them. It was funny to watch the people as they crumpled up various bills and rubbed them against the white wrapping paper. Fortunately for them, no one possessed any bad money.

"I guess yours was just a stray bill," Mr. Harper said to Bert and Nan. "It's too bad."

The twins left the store and hurried home. Mrs. Bobbsey was sorry to learn about the money, and said she was glad it was not more than five dollars. She quickly examined the money in her purse and sighed in relief when she found no more counterfeit bills.

At dinner that evening Mr. Bobbsey heard the story. At once he looked at the bills in his wallet but found they all were good United States money.

"I hope there's none of this counterfeit money in my office," he said. "I must look first thing in the morning. Well, children, tell me what you did today. Did anything else unusual happen to you?"

In reply, all the twins began to talk at once, and Daddy Bobbsey laughed heartily.

"One at a time, please. Suppose we start with my Little Fat Fairy," he said, beaming at Flossie. He loved to call her this, and she liked to hear him say it.

"Waggo brought home a kitten in his mouth," the little girl said. "We couldn't find her owner so Mother said we could keep her."

"Well, that's fine. After dinner you'll have to show her to me. And Freddie, my Little Fireman," he laughed, using his pet nickname for the small boy, "did anything happen to you today?"

"No, Daddy," his young son replied. "Maybe it should have, but it didn't."

Everyone laughed. Then Bert and Nan took turns telling their parents about having met Aunt Sallie Pry. They said that the elderly woman was going to the mansion of a Chinese named Sing Foo, and that perhaps she would take the twins there sometime.

"She said the place is kind of mysterious," stated Nan. "Do you know where it is, Daddy?"

Mr. Bobbsey said yes, he knew the place very well.

"Sing Foo is a retired circus performer," Mr. Bobbsey explained. "I believe he inherited a great deal of money from someone, so he left the circus and came to Lakeport. The place he bought had been for sale a long time. It's a very large house and no one seemed to want it."

The twins' father went on to say that Sing Foo had fixed the place up, furnishing it with beautiful Chinese furniture and works of art.

"Several years ago he allowed the public to come there and look at his home. It was a real show place, but as he grew older he became tired of this, and for some time he has not allowed the public to visit it."

"Does he have a lot of servants?" asked Flossie.

"I believe not," her father replied. "In fact, I think he lives alone."

"Then maybe that's why he asked Aunt Sallie Pry to come and take care of his home," said Nan.

Mr. Bobbsey looked thoughtful. "From what I can recall of the house, that would be a big job," he said. "Sing Foo had fish and birds all over the place."

Bert did not think these were very mysterious. "Aunt Sallie told us the house was mysterious," he remarked.

"I'm sure I don't know what she could have meant by that," Mr. Bobbsey replied. "But just to go through the old mansion gives one a spooky feeling."

"Oh, I hope we can go there," said Nan.

"I doubt that you can," Mrs. Bobbsey spoke up. "I believe Sing Foo had trouble with people breaking his lovely things. I'm sure he wouldn't want four lively children going through his house."

Nothing more was said on the subject that evening, but the twins hoped that in some way they could get out to the mysterious old mansion. It was bedtime before they knew it, and the next morning they had to go to school.

Bert and Nan did not expect to get home very

early that afternoon because their class was taking a hike in the woods. Danny Rugg, who was in the same grade, kept out of Bert's way. This was a good thing, because the Bobbsey boy was still provoked over what the bully had said to him in Harper's store about the counterfeit money.

Just before school closed, the teacher, Miss Moore, said the month's report cards were ready, but she was not going to give them to her pupils until the end of the afternoon.

"I'm afraid some of you might drop them in the woods," she stated, "so I shall carry them myself."

Although the walk had been planned to teach the children about various stones, they found many other things to interest them. Squirrels and rabbits scampered out of sight along the path, and birds twittered overhead. It was a beautiful day, and the boys and girls wished that they might go swimming in the lake near by.

As they came to a spot near the water, Miss Moore asked her pupils if they would like to have a treasure hunt. All were eager for this, so she suggested they sit down beside the lake while she hid some candy and cookies she had brought along. Nan happened to be standing near her, and Miss Moore asked the girl to hold the report cards.

Nan held them for a few moments. Then suddenly her attention was distracted by a loud screeching noise overhead. Looking up, she saw a blue jay and a squirrel in a fight on a tree limb. The blue jay was trying to peck out the squirrel's eyes!

"Oh!" cried Nan. "You mustn't do that!"

Without thinking, she laid the report cards on a stone and dashed forward to frighten the bird away. At this very moment a strong gust of wind came and blew the report cards helter-skelter.

"Oh, quick!" Miss Moore called out to the girl.

Nan Bobbsey turned around. Seeing what had happened, she ran back, but she was too late. The mischievous wind was carrying the cards toward the lake!

Several of them became buried by flying leaves. Four or five blew into the water!

CHAPTER III

A STRANGE PARTY

NAN was dreadfully upset. Bert rushed to her side at once, and so did several of the other boys and girls. They began running around trying to find the lost cards. Bert offered to wade into the lake, but Miss Moore would not let him do this.

"You might catch cold," she said. "We'll have to let those reports go."

After all the cards which could be found had been turned over to the teacher, she checked off the names of her pupils. Six reports still were missing. Unfortunately, one of these belonged to Danny Rugg. The bully could not resist taunting Nan.

"So the teacher's pet is in wrong," he said to her. "Maybe now you won't get such good marks."

"What do you mean?" cried Bert, coming to his twin's defense. "Miss Moore never gives Nan any better marks than she deserves."

"Oh, no?" said Danny with a sneer. "You just ask anybody." With this the unpleasant boy ran off.

Nan apologized to Miss Moore and asked what she might do to make up for the trouble she had caused. The kind woman patted the girl's shoulder and told her not to worry any more about it. Then, in a low voice she whispered:

"Really, Danny should thank you for losing his card. He has a very poor report this month."

Nan was not surprised to learn about Danny's standing in the class. The boy was lazy and always tried to avoid work of any kind.

The treasure hunt went on. As soon as all the candy and cookies had been found and eaten by the children, Miss Moore said they must start for home. It was growing late and they had a long way to go.

It was nearly six o'clock when Bert and Nan reached their house. They met Aunt Sallie Pry coming out of the front door. She told the Bobbseys she had just delivered a new dress which she had made for Flossie.

"She looks very sweet in it," the elderly woman said.

"I'm sure she does," Nan replied, and added, "Are you going to Sing Foo's?"

"No, I'm not going to sing," the old lady replied. "Why did you ask?"

The twins pursed their lips to keep from laughing at the deaf woman's mistake. Nan spol e loudly. "Are you going to Sing Foo's mansion?"

"The man's son isn't there. Sing Foo lives alone," Mrs. Pry answered.

The Bobbsey girl was almost discouraged trying to find out what she wanted to know. Sometimes Aunt Sallie seemed to hear pretty well, while at other times she scarcely seemed to understand what anyone was saying. Bert thought he would try to make her hear him, and said loudly:

"Are you going to take care of Sing Foo's house for him?"

"Yes, I am," Mrs. Pry replied. "I shall go there tomorrow morning to learn my duties."

The twins wanted to ask her if she thought the retired circus performer would let them come out to see his mysterious place, but they thought it best not to try this, since they had to shout so loudly. Everyone in the neighborhood would be sure to hear them!

After Aunt Sallie had gone on her way, Bert and Nan went inside the house. Daddy Bobbsey came home a few minutes later, and the family gathered in the living room awaiting Dinah's call to dinner. Nan related her mishap with the school report cards, and ended by telling what the teacher had said about Danny's marks being so low.

"It was sweet of Miss Moore to try making you feel better, Nan," Mrs. Bobbsey spoke up.

"Yes," her daughter agreed. "But if Danny had heard it, he probably would have called me teacher's pet again. I'm not that, am I, Bert?"

"Of course not," her brother replied. "Danny Rugg makes me so mad I sometimes feel like—"

"Like a bull," said Freddie.

The others laughed, but they knew why he had said this. Freddie had been to his Uncle Daniel's farm one time when a bull had got very mad and they had had a dreadful time with it. The small boy had almost been attacked by the mad animal.

Mrs. Bobbsey suggested that perhaps Bert was as mad as a March Hare.

"I heard Sam say he was as mad as hops one time," giggled Flossie.

"And I get mad as a hornet at times," laughed Daddy Bobbsey.

"And I get mad as a wet hen," put in Nan, recalling another well-known expression.

Bert said Danny made him mad enough to be as mad as all of the things they had mentioned, and more, too.

"I don't blame you," said Nan.

"Maybe some day I can teach him a lesson," the boy stated.

"Whatever you do, be careful, son, that you do not go too far," advised his father.

"I will, Dad," Bert promised. "But—"

"Dinner am served," a cheery voice broke in from the doorway. Dinah stood there in a crisp white apron, smiling at the Bobbsey family.

Freddie hopped from his chair and started as usual to make a beeline for the dining room. Mr. Bobbsey held him back, reminding his small son that Mother should go first.

After dinner the older twins sat down to do their home work. Flossie and Freddie went off to get ready for bed. Flossie decided to try on her new dress.

"It's so pretty," she thought, after she put it on and had turned round and round many times in front of a long mirror to look at herself. "This is really a party dress," she told herself. "Maybe I ought to have a party and wear it."

With this thought she went to bed, and had a funny dream. She could see herself sitting in a theater watching rows and rows of little girls on the stage. They all looked just like herself, and they all had on dresses exactly like her new one. When the little girls began to dance, it seemed to Flossie as if there were a hundred Flossie Bobbseys all doing the same thing.

In her dream Flossie tried to climb up to the stage, but she could not seem to do this. It bothered her so much that finally she cried out, and the next thing she knew her sister Nan was shaking her and saying:

"Flossie, Flossie. What's the matter?"

"I don't want there to be any other Flossie Bobbsey," said the small girl sleepily.

Nan thought this was a very strange thing for her to say, until Flossie explained what had happened in the dream. Nan told her sister to try not to think about anything, and then she would rest much better.

Flossie slept very well after that. But the subject of a party was strong in her mind. She did not know that an opportunity for one would come so soon, but it did the very next afternoon. She and Joan Johnson had walked home from school together and now stood in front of Joan's house talking. All of a sudden Joan gave a shout.

"Oh, Flossie! Look! Look! Is it—can he—Oh, my goodness, it is!"

Flossie Bobbsey wondered what her small chum was exclaiming about, but when she turned around as Joan had done, she knew. Running up the street toward them was the Johnsons' lost dog Sport. It did not seem possible that the animal was really home again.

"Sport! Sport!" cried Joan.

She got right down on the sidewalk and hugged her new-found pet. "Oh, you beautiful, wonderful old thing!" she half sobbed into the fur on his neck. "Where have you been?"

Flossie was sure the lovely old dog wished he could tell them, but all he could do was wag his tail and hold up his paw for them to shake.

Joan dashed into her house, followed by Flossie and Sport. She called loudly to her mother to come see the surprise. Mrs. Johnson was as glad to see Sport as her daughter had been. Many a time she had read stories about dogs being able to find their way home from long distances, but Sport had been gone so long she had given up hope of his ever returning. The woman picked him up and gave him a hug.

"Are you hungry?" she asked. "You come with me and I'll get something for you to eat."

After the excitement of the homecoming was over, Flossie said she must hurry along to her own house. As the little girl was about to leave, a thought came to her. Eagerly she turned to Joan and said:

"Let's have a party for your dog. Sport ought to get 'quainted with his old friends again."

"What kind of a party?" Joan wanted to know.

"A dog party, of course," Flossie replied. "We'll have it at my house. We'll invite Snap and Waggo and all the other dogs around here."

"How will they get to your house?" asked Joan.

Flossie had not thought of this. "I guess their owners will have to bring them," she decided.

It was arranged that Joan was to get in touch with a few of their friends and invite them and their dogs to the party. Flossie and Freddie would ask several others to bring their pets.

Flossie was so excited about the idea that she ran all the way home. She found Freddie playing in the back yard with his toy fire engine. Although the little boy had a great many toys, he did not like any of them so well as his fire engine. Flossie thought this probably was because it could squirt real water.

"Look out!" he cried, as his twin hurried toward him.

Flossie informed her brother if he dared to squirt any water on her she would not let him come to her party. At once Freddie shut off the nozzle of his hose and inquired what party she meant.

"It's a dog party in honor of Sport. Freddie, Sport came home today. What do you think of that?"

Freddie thought it was wonderful, of course, and he liked the idea of the dog party, too.

"I know what," he said suddenly. "Let's take the money out of our piggy banks and buy ice cream."

Flossie thought this was a splendid idea, but she

was inclined to think the animals would like dog biscuits better than ice cream. So it was decided they
would buy two kinds of refreshments.

"When are we going to have the party?" Freddie
wanted to know.

"Tomorrow afternoon," his twin replied. "On
our way home from school we'll buy things for it."
Then she added, "Freddie, put your fire engine away
and let's go invite our friends."

The little boy was agreeable to this, so a few
minutes later they started off. First they went to Ted
Blake's house and invited him and his collie dog
Laddie. Ted thought the party sounded like a lot
of fun.

The small Bobbsey twins next went to the home
of Susie Larker, and asked her to bring Rover, her
sheep dog. Then they spoke to Mary Wenton and
Harry Ford, telling them to bring their cocker span-
iels to the party.

"Maybe we ought to ask some of Bert's and Nan's
friends," Flossie suggested to Freddie. "Charlie
Mason has a nice setter. Let's go there."

"All right," agreed Freddie. "How about Nellie
Parks and her poodle?"

All the children who were invited eagerly accepted
the invitation. Flossie and Freddie did not mean to
be secretive about the party, but they were so busy
planning for it they forgot to mention it to anyone
else at the Bobbsey home. Their mother and father
had gone out of town for the evening, and Nan and
Bert had music lessons late that afternoon.

The small twins had their dinner alone. As soon as they finished eating, they went upstairs to empty their piggy banks and count the money. Flossie had stuffed a dollar bill into hers.

"I'd better see if it's real," she told Freddie.

Quickly she rubbed it against a piece of white writing paper to see if any green color would come off. She was relieved when some marks appeared on the sheet.

"It's good money," she told her brother, "and we can buy lots of ice cream with it."

The little twins could hardly wait for school to be over the following day. The minute they left the building they hurried to the stores. Flossie purchased the ice cream, while Freddie ran across the street to buy three boxes of dog biscuits.

"Will these be good for big dogs and little dogs?" he asked the man who waited on him.

"Yes, indeed," the storekeeper replied. "Give just one biscuit to your little dog and two to your big dog. But what do you want with three boxes? They'll last such a long time."

Freddie explained that he and his sister were giving a dog party. The man laughed heartily and said he hoped there would not be any trouble.

"What do you mean?" asked Freddie.

The storekeeper replied that he hoped all the dogs would get along with one another. "If they don't," he said, "just turn the hose on them."

Freddie thanked the man for his advice and said he would use his fire engine hose if there should be any trouble. As soon as he and Flossie got home the little boy brought his toy to the side of the house and filled it with water so as to be ready for an emergency.

"Here they come!" shouted Flossie half an hour later. She had been upstairs to put on the new party dress Aunt Sallie Pry had made for her.

Ted Blake, with Laddie on a leash, wanted to know whether the party would be indoors or on the lawn. Freddie and Flossie giggled. They had not thought of this. The question was settled by Bert and Nan, who returned from school at that moment.

"You say twelve dogs are coming!" cried Nan when she heard what was going on. "Well, of course they'll stay outdoors. They'd wreck our house."

Joan, Harry, Charlie, Mary, and half a dozen other children and their dogs arrived at the same time. The Bobbseys' old dog Snap, who had been brought out to the porch, gave one look and scratched on the door to be allowed to go back into the house.

"You're not a very nice host," Flossie scolded him. But she let him in nevertheless. After all, Snap was old and grouchy.

Young Waggo, the Bobbseys' fox terrier, evidently thought the party was a grand idea. He ran out onto the lawn and began barking at all his friends. Soon all the other dogs were barking and howling.

What a din!

Suddenly a scottie snarled loudly and tried to bite

Joan Johnson's dog Sport. This seemed to be a signal for all the animals to start fighting.

"Oh!" screamed Flossie. "What'll we do?"

"If we only had some food for them!" said Nan.

"We have!" cried Flossie, and dashed into the house for the dog biscuits.

Hurrying out, she tore off the lids from the three boxes of dog biscuits. Nan quickly threw the contents among the snarling dogs. They gobbled them up in a few moments and then began to fight all over again.

The young masters and mistresses of the animals tried pulling their pets away, but they had no success. When Mary Wenton was nipped on the leg, she cried out that the other children had better run, and they did.

Left to themselves, the dogs got into a dreadful free-for-all. The uproar was terrific. Neighbors came dashing from all the houses.

Freddie recalled what the man at the store had told him to do in case of trouble, so he set his toy fire engine to work, and squirted water on the animals. But the tiny stream seemed to make no impression on them, and they yapped and snapped worse than ever.

The children had scattered in every direction, and were shouting and crying out to their pets. The animals did not pay the least attention. Instead, they snarled, growled, and snapped ferociously at one another.

CHAPTER IV

THE MYSTERY MANSION

WHEN Dinah heard the uproar outside the Bobbsey house, she rushed from the kitchen to see what the trouble was. Looking out the front door, she gave a cry of horror.

"Oh, my goodness! Whatever has dose chilluns done?"

The loyal old cook tried to think what she could do to stop the fighting dogs. Seeing Freddie squirting water on them gave her an idea. She rushed to the telephone and called the fire department.

"Please bring yo' hose up here and drown all dese dogs," she said excitedly.

The man at the other end of the line asked her what in the world she was talking about.

"Dey's a hundred dogs fightin' on our lawn," replied Dinah. "Please send a hose right away and do somethin' about it."

Within three minutes the children outside heard the fire engine clanging up the street. They supposed there was a fire near by, and were greatly surprised when the engine stopped in front of the Bobbsey home and two men hopped out. They began to unreel a hose, and a few seconds later were playing a heavy stream of water on the fighting dogs. It was a very effective way to stop the battle. Dripping wet and confused, the animals slunk off to their homes.

"I—I guess my idea about a party wasn't so good," said Flossie to Nan when the excitement was over, "but maybe we'd better eat the ice cream."

"All right," agreed her sister, "but it's too wet to eat out here. You go tell our friends to come into the house. I'll get the plates ready."

Most of the children had started to go away, but when Flossie and Freddie called loudly to them to come back for refreshments, all except Mary Wenton returned. Mary thought she had better go home and have the wound on her leg attended to.

"I guess you're right," said Flossie. "I'm awful sorry about what happened."

The others enjoyed the ice cream and also some cookies which Dinah took out of a big crock. There was not enough milk in the house for all the children, but there were several bottles of soda, so in the end everyone had something to drink.

The dog party was talked about for days in Lakeport. There was even an article in the newspaper telling of it. Among those who read the item was Aunt Sallie Pry. When the elderly woman stopped at the Bobbsey house one day she asked about it. The twins told her the story in detail, then they inquired if she was still working for Sing Foo. Mrs. Pry replied that indeed she was, and that she had merely come into Lakeport to get more clothes.

"Sing Foo has to take a long trip," she said. "He has been called to San Francisco on business. I'm to take full charge of the house while he's gone."

"Oh, do you have to take care of all the birds and fish?" Flossie asked her loudly.

Mrs. Pry was surprised to learn that the little girl knew about them. The elderly woman answered that she was going to try taking care of them, although she knew it would be a big job for her.

"I asked Sing Foo if I might bring you out to see his place," she told the twins. "He'd be glad to have you come any time. Would you like to go?"

All the children were delighted at the invitation. Bert and Nan were a little more dignified in their acceptance than the small twins were. Freddie was so happy he turned a somersault and Flossie skipped about the room.

"When are we going?" the little girl wanted to know.

She had to repeat this three times before Aunt Sallie understood her. At last, however, the woman replied that they could go the following afternoon. Mr. Bobbsey said he would have Sam drive them out to Sing Foo's mansion and later call for them.

Promptly at four o'clock the next day the twins arrived at Sing Foo's mysterious house and rang the doorbell. For several minutes no one came to answer. Then finally an elderly Chinese opened the door.

"Welcome, little friends," he said, smiling and introducing himself as Sing Foo. He told them how glad he was they had come, and added, "Sunshine in hearts of little people make sunshine in hearts of old men."

The children liked him at once, but they clung together as they entered the large hall. It was a strange place indeed. In the dim light queer Oriental statues gazed at them.

"I'll tell Mrs. Pry you've come," said Sing Foo. "The good woman is trying to cook rice for me the way I like it." He smiled as he added, "A bowl of well-cooked rice is more good to a man than many nights of entertainment."

With this remark the Chinese vanished through a swinging door. The Bobbsey twins looked at one another. They wondered how Aunt Sallie was getting along in this strange place. Presently the kind old lady and her employer came into the hall.

"Leave your wraps here," the man directed the children, "and I will show you my house."

After they had taken off their sweaters, he opened the door to what the children supposed was the living room. It was a very large room filled to overflowing with objects of all kinds. Beautiful pictures hung on the walls, and on the floor was a heavy tan colored rug with small blue ships woven into it. Freddie sat down on the floor at once and tried to figure them out. He had never seen any sailboats like them and mentioned this fact to Sing Foo.

"They are Chinese junks," the man replied. "Chinese junks never go out of China, so you never see them here."

Nan was particularly interested in the carved furniture. She sat in one of the big chairs, and although she was tall for her age, her feet dangled over the edge.

As the Bobbsey twins went from room to room they saw many unusual and beautiful works of art. Freddie and Flossie finally grew tired of looking at them, and asked Sing Foo where he kept his birds and fish.

"They are in basement in very special room," the Chinese replied.

He promised to show them to the children later. This did not satisfy Freddie's curiosity, so he asked Sing Foo where he kept the things from the circus. The man laughed and replied that they were stored in the attic. Seeing the look of disappointment on the small boy's face, the Chinese offered to put on a little show for his guests.

"Please, if you will go to the room of the rug of ships, I will put on my magician's costume and do some tricks for you," the man said.

As the twins went there with Aunt Sallie, she told them that Sing Foo once had performed in the main part of a circus. He had been injured when he fell from a horse, and after that had become a magician in a side show. A few moments after the group had seated themselves, a voice spoke to them softly.

"I hope you will like me," it said.

The twins looked all around. They could see no one.

"Can you not find me?"

"No," said Bert.

"Look at the ceiling," the voice directed them.

The children gazed up but could see nothing. In a few moments they looked down again. There, standing right in front of them, was Sing Foo; at least, they thought this person must be Sing Foo, though he looked very different. The man had on a red robe with golden dragons embroidered on it. He wore a small matching hat with a long, black queue hanging down his back. Above his lips was a sweeping mustache, which made him look rather fierce.

"Oh, where did you come from?" cried Freddie.

"Where indeed?" asked the magician mysteriously.

He did not answer the children's question; instead, he held out his hands, palms up. They were empty. He closed them for a second. When he opened them again, two blue robins' eggs lay there. Freddie hopped from his chair and picked up one of them. It was real. He was not seeing things. But where had it come from?

The little boy put it back on Sing Foo's palm. The magician closed his hand, then opened it again. The eggs were gone!

Suddenly Flossie gave a little scream. She had seen something moving on the top of Sing Foo's hat. As the other children looked at her, she pointed. A little gray mouse was crawling slowly around the folds of the magician's hat. The man seemed to be entirely unaware of this.

"Is something the matter, little girl?" Sing Foo

asked in a deep voice, gazing at the excited child.

By this time the mouse was walking down the man's queue.

"It's on your braid!" Freddie cried out.

Sing Foo flipped his queue over his shoulder. Seeing the mouse, he looked at it, saying:

"Did Mrs. Pry let you out?" Looking at Bert, he continued, "Young man, would you like to have this for a pet?"

The Bobbsey boy thought he was supposed to say yes, though one never can be sure how to answer a magician's questions. So he said yes, he would like to take it home.

"Then come and pick it up," the man ordered.

Bert left his chair and walked forward, closing his hand over the little gray mouse. But to his amazement it was not there. He looked on Sing Foo's queue, robe, and hat. The tiny animal had vanished completely. The magician asked the boy what the trouble was.

"Don't you want the mouse?" Sing Foo asked.

Bert could see that the man's eyes were twinkling and that he was only teasing him. So Bert thought he too would have some fun. In his pocket he happened to have a dog biscuit. Reaching in, he pulled it out and laid it in Sing Foo's hand.

"Give this to your mouse if he gets hungry," the boy laughed, and then returned to his chair.

Sing Foo liked this. He smiled broadly and did not look fierce at all. In a moment the magician walked over to Flossie. He asked her whether she always took her baby with her when she went calling.

"I haven't any baby," said Flossie.

"But you have a doll baby," the magician said.

"Yes," admitted Flossie, "but I didn't bring her with me."

"Then how did this get here?" Sing Foo asked her, looking down at the seat of the large chair which Flossie only partly filled.

The little girl stared. The others looked too, and could not believe their eyes. Beside the child sat a large Chinese baby doll.

"Oh, how did she get here?" Flossie cried, picking up the adorable doll and hugging it.

Secretly she wished Sing Foo would give it to her, but she realized that probably he needed it in his magician's work. Suddenly the doll baby began to cry. Flossie immediately looked for a tiny key on its back. She had a baby doll at home which would cry when wound up. But this doll had no key.

Although Freddie and Flossie were mystified by the crying, Bert and Nan had caught on to the trick. Sing Foo was a ventriloquist! He could throw his voice and make it sound as if someone else were speaking or crying.

The man picked up the doll and carried it to a table. Then he came back to the little group and announced that he thought they must have had enough entertainment for one day.

"Oh, please go on," Freddie begged him. "I want to see all your tricks."

"I'm afraid I haven't many more," Sing Foo said. "But maybe my house will do some tricks for you."

The twins wondered what he meant by this, but they were not left in doubt long. Suddenly on the other side of the room a large chair began to rock all by itself!

CHAPTER V

MORE MYSTERY

THE Bobbsey twins stared in amazement! Aunt Sallie Pry began to feel a little uncomfortable. Being deaf, she had missed a great many of Sing Foo's remarks. Having things appear and disappear so strangely was very mystifying to her. Now, to see a chair rocking all by itself on the far side of the room was almost too much for her.

"Who—who is making the chair rock?" Flossie asked, a little frightened.

Sing Foo turned around, remarking that he did not see any chair rocking. This was true enough. The chair now was standing perfectly still.

"Please tell me what you mean," said Sing Foo. "Some time little girl think she see something she want to have happen?"

"Oh, I'm sure I saw that chair over there rock it-self," Flossie insisted.

Her sister and brothers agreed, as they had seen it too. Sing Foo told the little girl that perhaps if she spoke to the chair it might do it again for her.

So Flossie called out, "Rock, chair, rock!"

An instant later the old chair began to rock back

and forth violently. Bert, feeling sure the magician had caused this, watched the man very carefully instead of looking at the chair. But so far as he could see, Sing Foo was standing right where he had before and had done nothing.

"Maybe there's a black thread running from the back of the chair to his hand for him to pull," the Bobbsey boy thought, and went over to find out. But no thread was there. "Please make the chair rock again," he said to the magician.

The Chinese laughed. "Wise boy can think up many answers to tricks," he said. "Maybe wise boy can do trick also."

Before Bert could answer, Freddie called out, making the request that the chair rock once more. Immediately it obeyed. Then the magician insisted that his show was over. He pulled off his flowing mustache, and once more they could plainly see Sing Foo's kind, smiling face.

Aunt Sallie Pry and the Bobbseys left their seats and went over to examine the mysterious rocker. Sing Foo nodded to Bert and the boy followed him. When they were a little distance away from the others the magician whispered something to him. The lad's eyes opened wide and he grinned, promising Sing Foo that he would not tell anyone what he had just been told.

"I'll keep it a secret—at least until you come back from San Francisco," he said.

Nan walked over to the Chinese and asked him whether his house had any special name.

"When many visitors used to come here, I had a special name for my house," he explained, "but I never use it any more. What do you think I should call it?"

Nan laughed. "I think you ought to call it Mystery Mansion," she answered him.

It was the magician's turn to laugh now. He thought this was a very good name, and added in his philosophical way:

"House of mystery never grow dull."

"I'm sure this one never would be dull," said Nan. "May we see some more of your things?"

Sing Foo said he would show the children his tropical fish. He led the way to the basement. In one part of it a large room was fixed up almost like a little park. Short grass walks wound around pools of water. There were two small trees with benches beneath them on which people might sit. The children wondered how Sing Foo managed to make trees and grass grow in the basement, but presently they found out. He turned on a large ceiling light which shed warm rays just like sunshine over the whole scene.

When he did this the twins could see hundreds of fish playing around in the various pools. The fish were so beautiful the four Bobbseys got down on their knees near the water to see them better.

"Oo!" cried Flossie a moment later. "There's one that looks like an airplane!"

"And it can fly," said Sing Foo. "It is called 'Butterfly Fish.'"

"There goes one with a head like a bulldog," stated Freddie, chuckling. "His head is so big I don't see why he doesn't turn upside down."

"Nature takes care of everything," said Sing Foo.

He pointed out something floating on the surface of the water. The children thought it was a dead leaf, but when the Chinese touched it with a stick, suddenly a tiny head raised up and the "leaf" began to swim.

"Oh, it's a fish!" cried Flossie.

"Yes," said Sing Foo, "but not a nice fellow. He eats only other fish!"

"Then why do you leave him in this pond with all these beautiful fish?" Bert asked.

Sing Foo's eyes twinkled. "He is a coward; coward never attack something bigger than himself. I give the bad fellow very small fish to kill and eat. They are in a tank in another room. Come, I will show you."

Bert and Nan began to feel that there must be a great deal of work at Mystery Mansion. They wondered how Aunt Sallie ever was going to manage it all alone. The Chinese must have guessed their thoughts, because he said:

"Hungry fish and birds who cannot get own food must be fed regularly by human beings." Then he added suddenly, "Would the Bobbsey twins like to stay at Mystery Mansion?"

The twins were not sure that he was extending them an invitation. They thought it more likely he was trying to find out if they would be afraid to stay at his mysterious home. Bert and Nan promptly told him they thought the place was very beautiful and comfortable, even though it was full of secrets.

"I am glad Bobbsey twins are brave children," the delightful old Chinese smiled. "If Mrs. Pry gets lonesome while I am away, perhaps you will come here to keep her company, and help guard my secrets."

In a loud voice he repeated this to Aunt Sallie, who was looking into one of the pools. He added, "Would you like to have the twins out for a week end?"

"The fishes' fins come out in the deep end?" the woman asked in surprise.

Sing Foo smiled at the woman's mistake. Nan thought she could make Aunt Sallie understand better about Sing Foo's invitation than he could, so she shouted loudly:

"Do you think you will get lonesome here?"

Poor Mrs. Pry was still mixed up and said she did not know that fish ever get lonesome. It took several minutes to straighten her out, and when Aunt Sallie realized her mistake she laughed along with the others. The elderly woman admitted she not only might get lonesome, but also it would make it easier for her if she had someone to help her.

The Bobbsey twins thought it would be wonderful to stay at Mystery Mansion, and hoped their mother and father would let them accept the invitation.

"Come, I will show you my rare birds," Sing Foo offered.

But at this moment an automobile horn honked rather loudly, and the children knew Sam was outside to take them home. They hated to leave the fascinating place, and Freddie even said that Sam could wait while they looked at the birds. Nan advised her small brother that he had better go or perhaps he would not be allowed to come again. So grudgingly the little boy followed the others upstairs. Nan picked up their sweaters in the hall.

They all thanked Sing Foo for their lovely visit, then went out to the waiting automobile. The children hopped in and Sam started the motor. When they had gone about a quarter of a mile from Mystery Mansion, Nan suggested that they all put on their sweaters. It was then that they discovered Freddie's sweater was not in the car.

"I didn't put it with the others," the little boy admitted when they questioned him. "I laid it on a chair on the other side of the hall."

"Then we'll have to go back and get it," said Nan.

Sam turned the car around and returned to Sing Foo's home. Freddie hopped out, went up the porch steps and rang the doorbell. No one answered.

"Try it again," suggested Bert.

Freddie held his finger on the button a long time. The children could hear the bell very plainly, but no one came to the door.

"That's funny," said Nan. "Of course, Aunt Sallie can't hear the bell. But Sing Foo can."

Freddie kept on ringing for at least ten minutes, but the Chinese did not appear. The little boy looked disturbed. "How am I going to get my sweater?" he asked.

"I'll run around to the back," offered Bert.

But at the back door he had no better luck. The boy returned to the car to report this to the others. The Bobbsey twins stared at Mystery Mansion.

What could have happened inside it, they wondered.

CHAPTER VI

THE RUNAWAY

On their way home the Bobbsey twins continued to worry about what might have happened inside Mystery Mansion. When they reached their own house they spoke to their parents at once about it.

Mr. Bobbsey was inclined not to be concerned. He guessed that Sing Foo probably was feeding his birds and did not want to bother answering the bell. He reminded the children that the elderly man had kept the public from his place for some time past.

But Mrs. Bobbsey had a different idea. She went to the telephone and called the number of Mystery Mansion. When no one answered, she suggested they drive back to the place to be sure everything was all right. Her husband, after asking the children several questions, insisted that this would not be necessary.

"I feel sure nothing could have happened in the short time that the children left the house and returned to it for Freddie's sweater. We'll telephone later."

Freddie and Flossie, though too young to be really concerned, were still full of mystery. Just before go-

45

ing to bed, Freddie suggested to his twin that they get up very early the next morning and hunt for an adventure.

"All right," the little girl agreed. "If you wake up first, call me, and if I wake up first, I'll call you."

Freddie was the first one awake. He tiptoed to Flossie's room and whispered in her ear to get dressed. At first she did not understand what he meant; then suddenly Flossie remembered what she had promised to do.

"I'll get right up," she said.

"Meet me in the front hall," Freddie said softly, and then went back to his own room to get dressed.

Ten minutes later the little twins left the house together. No one else was up, not even Dinah, so not a person knew they had gone outside.

It was so early in the morning nobody was on the street. It was very quiet, and the small twins began to wonder whether they could find an adventure.

"What'll we do?" Flossie asked.

"I guess night is better for a mystery," Freddie conceded. "But I know something we *can* do."

He pointed down the street. Coming along at a slow pace was a milkman's wagon with two beautiful white horses pulling it. Most of the milk companies in Lakeport used small motor trucks, but old Mr. Jonathan Brown, who had been selling milk in town for forty years, still used horses.

"Let's ask the man if we can ride with him," suggested Freddie, starting to run down the street.

Flossie thought this would be fun. When they

reached the milk wagon the driver was just stepping out of it, a rack of bottles in his hand.

"Please, may we help you?" asked Freddie.

"I guess so. You're up early, aren't you?" the man asked, smiling. "Who are you?"

Freddie told him, and then asked the driver his name.

"Oh, just call me Tom," he replied. "I work for Mr. Jonathan Brown."

As Tom walked toward the back of the house where he was going to leave milk, Freddie and Flossie trotted along beside him. They chattered gaily, asking him which bottles contained milk and which held cream.

"Please, may we ride in your wagon with you for a little while?" Flossie spoke up, as they reached the street again.

Tom was not sure he should let the children do this, but Mr. Jonathan Brown had never told him he could not take passengers, so he figured probably it would be all right.

"O.K., come along with me," Tom said, "but you must sit very still and not get in my way."

The twins promised, and hopped into the milk wagon. Freddie wanted to hold the reins, but he was afraid to ask Tom if he might do this, for fear the man would refuse to let them ride with him. So he remained very quiet. The driver said "Giddap" to the horses, and they started off. They had gone only half a block when Tom pulled in the reins and the horses stopped again.

"Out we go," he said to the twins, stepping out of the wagon.

This time he allowed Freddie and Flossie to carry the rack of bottles between them. When they reached the back porch of the house to deliver the milk, he told the twins which bottles to take out and set in the doorway.

"This is lots of fun," said Freddie. "I'd like to be a milkman when I grow up."

Flossie giggled. Her twin always wanted to be something; a fireman, a detective, a cowboy, and now a milkman. She wondered if they were to go to Sing Foo's mansion whether Freddie would want to be a Chinaman! The little girl told Tom about their call at Mystery Mansion.

"Did you see the pagoda when you were there?" the milkman asked her.

"I don't know," she answered. "What is it?"

"A beautiful building on Sing Foo's estate. It's like buildings in China."

The twins said they had not seen it, and asked what was in it, but Tom did not know. He had heard, though, there were rare treasures inside.

"My goodness," the milkman said all of a sudden, "I'm forgetting my work. Whoa! Whoa!" he called to the horses.

Tom asked the twins if they would sit quietly in the wagon while he ran back to make a delivery at a house he had missed.

"Then I'll let you carry in the next order," he promised.

For several seconds the children sat still. Then suddenly Freddie said:

"I wonder if these horses would trot for me!"

Before Flossie could warn him not to try such a thing, her twin had said "Giddap." The horses started down the street. Freddie did not feel that he was doing anything naughty. The animals walked so slowly that Tom could catch up with them easily and hop onto the wagon, he was sure.

Ordinarily this might have been true. At this very moment, however, there came a loud wail from around the corner. It was from the siren on top of the Lakeport Fire Headquarters. Instantly the horses became frightened and started to gallop down the street.

"Oh!" shrieked Flossie. "Stop them!"

Freddie picked up the reins and pulled hard on them to stop the horses. But they paid no attention. Instead, the animals ran faster than ever. The milk wagon bounced up and down behind them as they raced along the bumpy pavement.

Freddie and Flossie were dreadfully frightened. They did not know what to do. Any instant they might be thrown out!

Reaching the corner, the horses swerved sharply into the next street. The milk wagon went around on two wheels, and for a couple of seconds it seemed as if it would overturn. But finally the wagon settled down on its four wheels, and the horses raced on.

Two blocks back was Nan Bobbsey. Having awakened and found her small sister missing, the girl had dressed and hurried from the house to look for Flossie. When she saw the milkman just returning to the street from making his delivery, she ran up to him.

"Pardon me," Nan said to the man, "but have you seen a little curly-haired girl around anywhere?"

For an instant Tom did not reply. He stared vacantly down the street. Then he startled the Bobbsey girl by saying:

"She—she's gone! She was in my milk wagon. The children must have driven off!"

"Children?" Nan repeated.

"Yes, there was a little boy with her," Tom said.

"That must be my brother Freddie!" Nan exclaimed. "Where are they?"

"I don't know!" the driver said, starting to run down the street.

Nan followed him. Turning the corner, the two of them gazed ahead. In the distance was the runaway!

"Oh!" cried Nan.

Tom was speechless. He finally mumbled a few words about knowing he should not have let the children ride with him, and took up the chase. Nan raced beside him, her heart pounding in fright. They never could catch up with the horses!

A quarter of a mile beyond, Tom and Nan could see railroad tracks. Evidently the horses were going to cross them! Nan's heart sank.

Suppose a train should come along!

CHAPTER VII

A RESCUE

NAN was in terror about what might happen to Freddie and Flossie. The runaway was bad enough, but if a train—

"What time is it?" she asked Tom excitedly.

"About seven o'clock," the man replied. "Why?"

"A train is due at Lakeport in five minutes!" the girl cried.

Once her father had had to catch this very train, and she had driven down to the station with him.

"Oh, I must do something!" Nan thought. "But what?"

Coming up a side street was an empty taxicab. Quickly she called to the driver, who stopped. Pulling open the cab door, the girl hopped inside, followed by the milkman Tom. Nan told the driver to race up the street as fast as he could. In the distance a train whistle shrilled.

"We have to stop that runaway before the train comes!" Nan cried. "Oh, please hurry!"

Tom was too frightened to say anything. He was quite sure he never would drive a milk wagon again if anything should happen to the small Bobbsey twins.

Coming up the road on the other side of the tracks was an automobile. The man at the wheel was hurrying to get to the Lakeport station. Suddenly he realized that the two galloping horses, which were coming toward him, were out of control. At first he thought no one was in the jostling wagon, but upon looking more intently he could see the heads of two small children.

"I must stop that runaway!" the man thought quickly.

With a burst of speed he crossed the tracks, jammed on the brakes of his car, and jumped out. Then he stepped into the path of the oncoming horses, and waved his hands back and forth in mid-air.

By this time the animals were almost upon him. Leaping up high, the man grabbed the bridles of the two horses and swung himself around the pole between them.

"Whoa!" he called. "Whoa!"

The animals slackened their speed a little but did not stop. Half a mile down the track the train whistle blew insistently.

Using all his strength, the man pulled himself up the pole onto the back of one of the horses and grabbed the reins. Then with full force he yanked hard on the left one. The animals, knowing someone used to handling horses was in charge, obeyed his signal. They reared slightly, but turned to the left just as the train roared noisily past the crossing.

At this moment the taxicab arrived at the spot. Nan and Tom jumped out. They gazed at the man who had saved the lives of the small Bobbsey twins.

"Sing Foo!" the girl cried.

As the Chinese leaped to the ground, she rushed up and hugged him. "Oh, how can we ever thank you?" she sobbed.

Sing Foo was pretty shaken himself. He had not been at all sure he was going to accomplish what he intended. The milkman tremblingly shook the rescuer's hand, but was too overcome to say anything more than "Thank you."

Freddie and Flossie climbed down from the wagon. Both of them, white and shaky, clung tightly to Nan. The only person in the group who could find much of anything to say was the taxicab driver. He was a very gruff fellow and began to scold everybody.

"Don't you know better than to leave kids alone in your wagon?" he shouted at Tom.

"You kids think you're grown up, don't you?" he yelled at Freddie and Flossie. "The idea of trying to drive big horses yourselves!"

Even Sing Foo came in for a rebuke. "What were you trying to do?" the taximan cried. "Get yourself killed?"

The reprimands brought all of them out of their silence. Sing Foo was the first to reply to the driver. In dignified tones he said:

"Lives of fine twins worth two of old man!"

The Chinese reached into a pocket, took out some money, and handed it to the taximan. He told the fellow he need stay no longer, adding that he himself would take the children home.

The Bobbseys climbed into his car. As Nan sat down on the back seat, she noticed a suitcase on the floor.

"Oh, Sing Foo, were you going to catch that train?" she asked.

The kindly Chinese confessed that he had planned to, but it would make no difference to him if he were to take a later train.

"There are many trains," he smiled, as he drove off, "but not many opportunities to be of service."

On the way to the Bobbsey house the twins were very quiet for a while, then Nan spoke up, telling Sing Foo how they had come back to Mystery Mansion the previous evening to get Freddie's sweater.

"No one came to the door when we rang the bell," she said. "We were afraid something might have happened to you or Mrs. Pry."

The Chinese smiled. "No, nothing happened," he assured her. "I told this to your father last evening. I had gone to the pagoda."

Pagoda! Flossie wanted to ask him what was inside the building, but at this moment they reached the Bobbsey home and Nan spoke up before the little girl had a chance.

"Please come in and meet our mother and father," Nan invited Sing Foo.

The modest Chinese did not want to be thanked

by them, but at the children's insistence he finally went inside.

Freddie hoped that nothing would be said about the dreadful thing he had done. But on thinking it over, he decided to tell his mother and father exactly what had happened.

Mr. and Mrs. Bobbsey were aghast when they heard the story, and thanked Sing Foo over and over again for his wonderful rescue of the little twins. When they learned from Nan he had missed his train, they said they were sorry about this.

"Were you on your way to San Francisco?" the children's father asked him.

The Chinese admitted that he had been, but added quickly that he was sure he could get a reservation on another westbound train. Mr. Bobbsey said the least he could do would be to make the arrangements for Sing Foo, and immediately put in a telephone call. Fortunately, he was able to get a reservation for the Chinese a little later.

After all the excitement was over, Mrs. Bobbsey said she thought they should sit down quietly and have breakfast. Sing Foo said he had had his, but he would talk with the others while they were eating.

"Maybe he doesn't like our kind of food," Flossie whispered to her mother, as they were going into the dining room.

"It happens that we are having rice pancakes for breakfast," Mrs. Bobbsey announced, turning to Sing Foo. "Have you ever eaten them?"

The guest replied he never had, and he believed

he would like to try them. After tasting one, he declared it was delicious. Dinah, who was passing a second plateful around the table, beamed with pleasure. The Negro cook felt very proud to serve something new in a rice dish to a man from a country where rice was used in so many different ways!

Flossie and Freddie hoped Sing Foo would perform some of his magic tricks for them, but they realized he must be too tired after his exciting morning. And no doubt his costume was at home anyway, so they said nothing. The Chinese did bring up the subject of Mystery Mansion, however.

"I hope Mrs. Pry can get along all right while I am away," he said. "Feeding hungry birds and fish takes much time."

Sing Foo did not say anything about the twins visiting Aunt Sallie until he was ready to leave the house. Then, as they were walking to his car with him, he remarked with a smile:

"Maybe Sing Foo's birds and fish will get lonesome as well as Mrs. Pry. You children must go out there soon."

"Oh, we'd love to!" cried Nan, while Bert, Freddie and Flossie all said in one breath, "We sure will!"

The magician started his car, waved his hand, and drove a few feet down the street. Then he stopped abruptly and called to the twins, who were still standing at the curbstone. He beckoned for them to come forward.

"I forgot to tell you something," Sing Foo whispered. "Mystery Mansion has many more secrets. Some are locked up with the Golden Key. Twins must find the key if they wish to see them."

Then, with a twinkle in his eyes, the Chinese drove off down the street.

CHAPTER VIII

THE MISSING KITTEN

"I WISH we could go to Mystery Mansion today," sighed Flossie, as she ran beside Nan on their way to school.

The twins found it necessary to hurry because the excitement of the early morning had taken a great deal of time.

"It would be fun," Nan agreed. "But if we go at all I guess it will have to be for a week end."

Every once in a while during school hours each of the Bobbsey twins found his mind wandering from his studies. How wonderful it would be out at Sing Foo's place! Bert kept recalling the secret the elderly Chinese had told him, and was eager to get out to the Mansion to look for something.

"And I hope I can find the Golden Key, too," the boy said to himself.

"Bert Bobbsey, what is the capital of Greece?" someone said sharply.

Coming to with a start, he stood up beside his seat in the classroom, looking very confused. Bert had not heard exactly what his teacher, Miss Moore, had asked him. Not far away Danny Rugg began to snicker. It always pleased him whenever the Bobbseys failed in anything.

"I'm sorry, Miss Moore, but I didn't hear your question," Bert confessed.

"What is the capital of Greece?" the teacher repeated.

Quickly the boy replied that it is Athens. He decided he had better pay strict attention from now on, and did so until the final bell rang.

After school Bert hurried over to his father's office, because he had promised to do some work there. The lad found the place in a state of excitement. Upon inquiring what the trouble was, he learned that during the morning Miss Munson, the young woman cashier, had taken in a counterfeit five-dollar bill. She had just discovered the mistake.

"I don't know how I ever happened to do such a thing," she told Mr. Bobbsey.

Bert's father asked Miss Munson if she could remember what the man who had given it to her looked like. It was just possible he was a counterfeiter!

"Oh, he looked like a workingman," the young woman replied. "He had on overalls and a peaked cap pulled down low on his forehead."

"Would you know him if you should see him again?" Mr. Bobbsey asked her.

"I can't say for certain," Miss Munson replied.

"Then you didn't recognize him as anyone who had ever been here before?"

Miss Munson said she had never seen the man previously. She looked at her order slips and found that the man had bought one heavy board. He had not given his name.

"The order slip isn't much of a clue, is it, Dad?" Bert asked.

"I'm afraid not, son. Well, we'll just have to forget the five dollars."

When Bert learned that the board had cost two dollars and fifty cents, he remarked to his father that really he was out the board and two dollars and fifty cents besides.

"That's right, son," Mr. Bobbsey agreed. "We gave the stranger two dollars and fifty cents in change as well as the piece of lumber."

The police were notified, and a detective was sent over to Mr. Bobbsey's office at once to make an investigation. He told those present a rather startling story.

"We learned there was a group of counterfeiters using an empty garage here in Lakeport, and we almost caught them. But unfortunately they skipped out just before we could nab them," the policeman said. "Now we can't seem to find a single trace of the men."

"Then you have no idea how far away they went?" Mr. Bobbsey asked.

The detective said it had been impossible to learn this. He added that the printing press the counterfeiters used in making fake bills had vanished also.

"Do you suppose one of the men bought a piece of lumber from my Dad?" Bert asked.

"It's possible," the detective replied. "And if he did, he may not be far away. But I hardly think that's the case. We had a tip from the police in a town about a hundred miles from here that a suspicious-looking truck had gone through there yesterday. The authorities are trying to trace it, for they feel pretty sure the counterfeiters and their printing press were in the truck."

After the detective left, Bert worked around the lumber yard. In the meantime the other Bobbsey children had gone directly home from school. Flossie, eager to play with the new kitten, looked about for her and found her in the kitchen. She was asleep in her basket. Friendly Waggo wanted to play with her, too, but the little gray cat did not wish to be disturbed. She yawned, put out a paw to push the dog away, and then closed her eyes again.

"You're an old sleepy head," said Flossie. "You need exercise."

The little girl picked up the kitten and carried her into the dining room. Behind them came Freddie, banging the door. Seeing the pet in his sister's arms, he called out flippantly:

"Hi, cat!"

The way he said it made Flossie realize they had not given their new kitten a name. So many things had happened during the past few days no one had thought of doing this. She spoke to Freddie about it.

"I guess we ought to call her Tramp, because she didn't have any home," he replied.

"That's not a very nice name," objected Flossie.

"She's so pretty she ought to have a pretty name." A moment later the little girl had an inspiration. "Her name ought to have something to do with gray because she's gray. What's gray?" she asked her twin.

Freddie thought for several seconds before answering. There were gray clouds, and gray eyes, and gray hair, but none of these would be a good name for a kitten, he felt sure.

"Oh, I know!" cried Flossie. "Smoke is gray. Why don't we call her Smoky?"

Freddie agreed this was an excellent name. He went close to the kitten, held her ears between his fingers, and said:

"You're Smoky!"

The little animal at once jumped down from Flossie's arms and walked off. The twins wondered if she had done this because she did not like her new name. As a matter of fact, the kitten was not thinking about her new name at all. She had spied something with which she wanted to play.

Jumping to the window sill, Smoky began to bat the pull cord on the shade. As it swung back and forth she gently tapped it, first with one front paw, then the other. This went on for a few moments, then the kitten must have given the cord a little tug, because suddenly the shade rolled up with a loud bang.

Freddie and Flossie laughed outright, but stopped almost at once, because the shade fell from the brackets and crashed to the table below. It hit a bowl of ivy, smashing the glass into several pieces. As the water from it began to run down the side of the table to the floor, Smoky gave a great leap from the window and hid under the buffet.

"Oh, you naughty kitten!" cried Flossie. "What will Mother say?"

As the little girl reached for her, the kitten ran into the hall, and neither she nor Freddie could find her. They got a rag, the dust pan, and a broom to clean up the mess. Dinah found another bowl for the ivy and set it on the table.

This seemed to be a day of mischief for Smoky. After the twins had gone upstairs, the kitten came out of hiding and started to investigate. She spied a basket of knitting materials which Mrs. Bobbsey had left in the corner of a living-room chair. Smoky jumped up to the seat and worked at the basket until she pulled out one of the balls of yarn. It was attached to a sweater being made for Nan.

The ball tumbled to the floor and rolled several feet away from the chair. Smoky must have thought the bright yellow worsted was a nice toy, because she rolled the yarn across the floor with her paw. She kept on through the door, down the hall, and into the dining room, leaving a long, yellow thread behind her.

Smoky played with the ball of yarn for some time, and no one came to stop her. Then Nan, walking into the house through the kitchen, came upon a strange scene in the dining room.

"Oh, my goodness!" she cried out.

The floor looked as if giant yellow cobwebs had been stretched all over it. Strings of worsted went criss-cross from leg to leg of chairs, tables, the buffet, and the tea table. It did not occur to the girl that Smoky had been the cause of all this, because the pet was not in sight. She thought probably Flossie or Freddie had been playing some game, and called upstairs to them.

When the little twins came down, they were as amazed to see what had happened as their older sister had been. They all concluded, however, that Smoky had been the cause of the trouble.

"I'll have to give her a good scolding," stated Flossie, speaking like a little mother. "Smoky, where are you?"

The gray kitten could not be found. The children looked in every place they could think of, but the cat was not anywhere around.

"She must have run away because she knew she was naughty," concluded Flossie.

"I don't see how in the world she could get out of the house," objected Nan. "I'm sure she's here, but I'm afraid she may be in trouble."

CHAPTER IX

A FALSE RUMOR

WHEN Bert and his father arrived that evening, they told the others about the fake five-dollar bill in Mr. Bobbsey's office, and how the detective had said some counterfeiters had almost been caught in Lakeport.

"But the men got away and took their printing press with them," the children's father stated.

"That's too bad," said Mrs. Bobbsey. "I certainly hope the police catch them soon. Fake money can cause a lot of trouble."

"And we have enough trouble here already," spoke up Flossie.

"We have?" said her father.

The little girl told him about the missing kitten, and how they had looked everywhere for her; under the furniture, in the closets, down the cellar, and up in the attic.

"You're sure she's in the house?" asked Mr. Bobbsey.

Flossie nodded. "And we'd just given her a name, too. Smoky."

"Smoky?" said Bert. Then he grinned. "Maybe

this is no time to make jokes," he remarked, "but perhaps she turned into smoke and went up the chimney!"

This gave the others an idea. They promptly looked up the chimneys of all the fireplaces in the house, but the little gray kitten was not in any of them. Flossie was sad. Her father tried to console her by saying young animals know how to take care of themselves better than most people think they can.

"So don't worry any more about Smoky, please," he told the children. "Let's have dinner. I'm starving. Isn't anybody else hungry?"

The family had barely seated themselves at the table when they heard a shout in the kitchen. Then Dinah called out:

"Oh, lawsy me. Oh, lawsy me! What next is gwine happen in dis yere house?"

The entire Bobbsey family left their chairs and rushed into the kitchen to see what was the matter. The cook was stooping over, reaching into the oven. A second later she pulled out a little gray kitten.

"Smoky!" yelled Flossie, and rushed forward to take the pet in her arms.

Dinah explained she had opened the oven door expecting to put in a pan of rolls to warm. To her surprise, she had seen the missing kitten crouching way back in a corner.

"How did she get in there?" exclaimed Mrs. Bobbsey. "Why, she might have been cooked to a crisp!"

The children shuddered at this thought, and declared then and there that they never would light an oven until first looking inside of it. Flossie put Smoky in her basket and carried it to the dining room. The little girl insisted upon having it right alongside her and forgot completely that she had planned to punish Smoky for having broken the bowl and ruined Nan's sweater.

The Bobbsey family had just finished eating when the telephone rang. The call was for Bert and was from Charlie Mason.

"Say, what's this I hear about your father passing out counterfeit money?" Charlie asked.

Bert Bobbsey thought he had misunderstood his friend. "What's that you say?" he questioned.

"There's a story going around town that your father is giving out counterfeit money," Charlie repeated.

"But that's not true!" the Bobbsey boy exclaimed. "You know my father wouldn't give out bad money, Charlie."

"That's what I thought," said his friend.

He went on to explain that his mother had been down to the butcher shop that afternoon and someone there had asked her if she had heard the story about Mr. Bobbsey. Then Charlie himself had gone in to get a soda at the candy store, and had been told the same thing. Later, when Mr. Mason had come home, he had said a man at the tailor's had repeated the story to him.

"Gee, this is awful," said Bert. "What really hap-

pened, Charlie, is that my father's cashier, Miss
Munson, took in a five-dollar counterfeit bill today.
But I'm sure Dad didn't give out any, unless—" He
paused a moment. "Say, Charlie, I'll call you back,"
he added quickly.

The Bobbsey boy hung up and rushed off to find
his father. Excitedly he told him what Charlie had
just said, and asked Mr. Bobbsey whether by any
chance he might have received other counterfeit
money and given it to shopkeepers by mistake.

"If I did, Bert, it was not intentional," his father
said, becoming concerned at once. "But this is a bad
state of affairs. I must track down the story right
away."

He asked Bert to find out from Charlie the names
of the shops where the Masons had heard the story.
Bert did this. He also learned that the only store
that would be open that evening was the candy store.
Unfortunately, the boy who had spoken to Charlie
at that place was not at work.

Mr. Bobbsey sighed. "The matter will have to
wait until morning, then," he said. "There's nothing
more to do about it now."

Bert, however, was not satisfied to let things rest
as they were. The more the Bobbsey boy thought
about it, the more convinced he became that someone had started the story just to make trouble for
his father. Suddenly he had an idea as to who the
person might be.

"Danny Rugg!" he decided, recalling his own ex-
perience with the counterfeit money at Harper's.

"That mean boy told everybody in the store I was trying to pass bad money. I'll bet Danny heard what happened in Dad's office today, and he just made up the story and told it to a lot of people."

Determined to find out, Bert got up early the next morning and hurried downtown. First he went into the butcher shop and asked the man who it was that had told him the story about Mr. Bobbsey passing bad money.

"Why, two women standing near the counter late yesterday afternoon were discussing it," the butcher replied. "Let me see now who they were. Oh, yes, one was Mrs. Smith and the other—hanged if I know, son. I can't remember her name."

Bert decided to take a chance. "Was she—was she Mrs. Rugg, do you know?"

"Why, come to think of it, I believe she was," the man said, scratching his head thoughtfully.

This was all Bert wanted to know. He thanked the butcher and left the store. Next he went to the tailor's shop. He learned from the man there that a boy who had called for his father's suit the afternoon before had told him to be careful about taking any money Mr. Bobbsey might give him.

"Who was the boy?" demanded Bert.

He expected to be told he was Danny Rugg, but this was not the case. He turned out to be a Jimmy Lasser. Bert did not know the lad, but he was pretty sure he was one of Danny Rugg's playmates.

Before returning home, Bert stopped at the soda shop where Charlie Mason had been told the story of the counterfeit money. From the boy there he learned two girls had warned him to be very watchful if he should be handed any bills by Mr. Bobbsey or members of his family.

The soda clerk did not know the names of the girls, but he had overheard one of them say that the fellow who had told them about it never had liked the Bobbseys. Bert left the shop, feeling sure the fellow was Danny Rugg. As far as he knew, Danny was the only person who had a grudge against him and his family.

When Bert reached home, the Bobbseys were having breakfast. Eagerly they listened to the boy's report.

"Thank you very much, son," said his father, after hearing it. "I'm inclined to agree with you that someone started the story to make things difficult for me. You say that at none of the stores the shopkeepers received any counterfeit money?"

"Not one," Bert replied. "They had only been told the story."

Although the Bobbsey family was worried because they did not want anyone in town to believe they would do such a thing intentionally, they were relieved that the tale was no worse. Bert could not forget his suspicion, and determined to seek out Danny Rugg after school and learn what he could from him.

When classes were over that day, he followed the bully from the building. Danny must have known Bert had something on his mind, because he hurried off as fast as he could. Bert Bobbsey ran after him.

"I want to talk to you," he said.

"Well, I don't want to talk to you. I have to go some place," snapped the rude boy.

Bert was not going to let him get away so easily. He hurried along beside Danny. Making up his mind to take a chance, Bert asked him abruptly:

"What do you mean by telling a story around town that my father is trying to pass bad money?"

"Who said I did that?" Danny argued.

"I've been investigating," Bert replied.

For a moment Danny looked scared. Then he assumed his usual attitude of bluff. "I don't know what you're talking about, but it wouldn't surprise me to hear that your father tried to pass a bad bill. You did, didn't you? And your sister threw some of the report cards in the lake, too."

"She did not!" Bert cried, furious. "You know very well the wind blew them there."

"That's her story," Danny sneered. "But I saw what happened."

Before Bert could argue the matter further, Danny suddenly turned into the walk of a house where an aunt of his lived, ran up the porch steps, and vanished inside. The Bobbsey boy stood there a moment, then started home. He was annoyed with himself.

"I didn't find out one single thing," he said to himself. "I guess I'm not much of a detective."

He was sorry not to be able to give his father a good report on locating the person who might have started the story. The boy still felt sure that Danny Rugg was the culprit, and he meant to get a confession from the bully some day.

The attention of the twins was turned to a more pleasant subject by a letter which had arrived that afternoon. It was addressed to Mrs. Bobbsey but directly concerned her children.

"It's from Mrs. Pry," she announced. "And it's an invitation."

"Oh, are we going to Mystery Mansion?" cried Flossie. "Then I can see the paggody."

"Mrs. Pry wants you to come there this week end," Mrs. Bobbsey replied. "And if you go, I suppose you will see the pagoda. But I'll have to talk the matter over with your father."

"Then it's all right with you, is it?" Bert asked his mother eagerly.

Mrs. Bobbsey smiled at her son, saying she believed he and Nan were dependable children, and furthermore, would look after their young brother and sister.

"I know Mrs. Pry will see that you have plenty of good food, and I'm sure you can be of great help to her."

Bert and Nan were glad Mrs. Bobbsey had not mentioned that they might encounter anything dangerous at Mystery Mansion. Sing Foo had said the place was full of secrets, and they wondered what might happen to them while trying to uncover the mysteries.

"Where do you suppose the Golden Key is?" Nan

said to her twin. "If it's too well hidden, maybe we won't be able to find it and unlock the secrets."

"I hope it won't take so much time to feed the fish and birds that we shan't have any left to look for the key," Bert replied.

All the children eagerly awaited Mr. Bobbsey's decision in the matter, and were thrilled when he gave his consent to the week-end visit with Aunt Sallie Pry.

"How would you like Sam to pick you up at school on Friday afternoon?" he asked.

The older twins and Freddie thought this was a fine idea; but to their surprise, Flossie did not want to do this.

"I'd rather come home first," she announced.

"But why?" Nan wanted to know.

Flossie was very mysterious. She would give no reason, and the others could not talk her into consenting to go early. Mrs. Bobbsey settled the matter by saying it would not make half an hour's difference, anyway, so if it would please the little girl, why not let her have her own way?

When the little twins were alone, Freddie tried his best to find out what Flossie had in mind. But though she usually told her little brother everything, this time she refused.

"It's a secret," was all she would say. "It's my own private secret."

CHAPTER X

THE WHISTLE

ON Thursday evening the Bobbsey twins packed their bags for the week-end trip to Mystery Mansion. Their mother had thought one suitcase for the boys and one for the girls would be enough, but again Flossie wanted things another way.

"Please, Mother, I'd like to take my own bag and I'd like to pack it all by myself," she said. "You want me to do things for myself, don't you?"

Mrs. Bobbsey smiled at her small daughter's whim, and replied that of course she wanted Flossie to learn to do things for herself. She named a few necessary articles, such as a toothbrush, a sweater, and rubbers, just to be sure that the little girl would not miss putting them into her bag.

When no one was looking Flossie made a trip to the kitchen. She got a paper bag and put several kinds of food into it. Then, carrying it upstairs, she hid the bag under some of the clothes in her suitcase. The little girl hoped that while she was at school the following day, neither her mother nor Dinah would look among her things.

Flossie need not have worried. Mrs. Bobbsey

spent most of the day helping to put on an entertainment at the Home for the Aged, and Dinah was very busy with her cleaning.

When school was over Flossie ran every step of the way to the Bobbsey house. She still had something to do before she could leave home for Mystery Mansion. From a closet she got a pasteboard box and hurried off to fill it and tie it up.

"I hope nobody stops me from taking this," she said to herself. "I shan't have nearly so much fun at Mystery Mansion if I have to leave the box home."

The other twins arrived a little later, and within fifteen minutes were ready to start. Sam already was waiting. Flossie had asked him to open the baggage compartment of the car and put in her suitcase and the mysterious box. The other bags were stored away quickly and the children hopped into the automobile. Dinah came outside to bid them good-by.

"Yo' better take dis along," she said, smiling, and handed a large covered basket to Sam. "I put a few odds and ends o' food in dere. Mebbe dey'll come in handy."

The children giggled. The basket was so large they knew the few odds and ends probably included a roast chicken, some homemade bread, a fluffy cake, and enough fruit for a week.

"Oh, thank you, Dinah," said Nan, as they started off, and Bert added:

"We sure won't starve."

Flossie smiled to herself. Maybe she need not

have put the little bag of food in her suitcase after all!

When the group reached Mystery Mansion, Sam tooted his horn and Bert pressed the doorbell. They had expected Aunt Sallie Pry to be awaiting them, but she was not about and she did not come to the door.

"Maybe she didn't expect us so early," said Flossie.

The little girl ran around to the back door and pounded on it loudly. Still Aunt Sallie did not come to let them in.

After each of the twins had tried for nearly fifteen minutes to make the woman hear and could get no response, they became worried. Had Aunt Sallie gone away, forgetting that they were to come? Or had something happened to her inside Mystery Mansion? The children talked matters over with Sam, and finally decided that they ought to go inside the house and investigate.

"But how can we?" asked Nan.

"Let's try the windows," Bert suggested.

Sam hoisted the lad to his shoulders and in this way each window on the first floor was examined. Not one of them was unlocked.

"Oh, what shall we do?" exclaimed Nan.

Bert looked upward. "There's a window open on the second floor. I wonder if I could get inside that way."

The others gazed at it, but could not figure out how he might reach the open window. Of one thing they all were sure; Mrs. Pry was too careful a housekeeper to go away and leave a window open. Therefore, she must be inside the Mansion.

"Something must have happened to Aunt Sallie," Nan told herself.

In circling the house a third time the children noticed a basement door, half hidden behind vines, which they had not seen before. Bert tried it, and to his delight found the door unlocked.

"Yo' all better let me go in first," said Sam. "If dere's any trouble inside, I don't want yo' all messin' wid it."

The elderly Negro pushed the door wide open and entered a dark and narrow corridor. He went only a few feet before coming to another door. This one was locked, but he pounded on it loudly. To his amazement it was opened almost at once.

Mrs. Pry!

"Sam!" the woman cried. "My goodness, why did you come to this door?"

The twins, who had been close on the man's heels, pushed ahead of him. Relieved to see Aunt Sallie all right, they began asking her questions. She could make neither head nor tail of what they were saying. Nan begged the other children to be quiet for a moment so she could explain.

"We rang at the door again and again," she said.

Mrs. Pry said she was very sorry she had not heard them.

"I've been feeding the birds down here," she explained, and showed the twins several small cages which they had not seen on their previous trip.

"It seems to me as if I never get through," the woman went on. "I think there must be over a hundred birds here."

"How many fishes?" Freddie asked.

"How many dishes? They all have dishes," Aunt Sallie answered.

Freddie smiled, and let it go at that. The woman led the children upstairs to the second floor and showed them where they were to sleep. Nan and Flossie would share one of the bedrooms. Bert and Freddie would sleep directly across the hall.

"My room is there," Aunt Sallie added, pointing to one which connected with that of Nan and Flossie.

"They're awfully big," said Flossie.

Sam said he would bring up the suitcases if they would show him how to get down to the front door. The twins laughed. They wondered themselves where this particular staircase was, and appealed to Aunt Sallie. She led them around two corners and showed them the steps.

"I'm going, too," said Flossie, and skipped down after the old Negro.

When Sam opened the baggage compartment he handed the little girl the white box she had brought along. Carefully Flossie carried it up to her new room and hid it under the bed. Not until Sam had driven off and the girls were unpacking their bags did the small twin bring her secret package out and open it.

"I hope she's all right," Flossie said, more to herself than to anyone else.

"Who's all right?" Nan questioned her.

"My precious darling," her small sister replied.

Nan stared as Flossie untied the cord on the box and took off the lid. Gently she lifted out her secret.

"Smoky!" cried Nan.

The kitten, glad to be freed from her box prison, leaped from her small mistress's arms and scampered out the bedroom door. Nan dashed after her.

"Oh, we mustn't let her get away!" she exclaimed. "She may harm the fish or the birds!"

Suddenly Flossie felt very bad. All the while she had been planning to give Smoky a trip to Mystery Mansion she had never once thought of Sing Foo's pets. She knew that cats often harm fish and birds, and sometimes even eat them!

Bert and Freddie had heard the commotion and now came to find out what the trouble was. Upon learning that Smoky was loose in the house, they also began a frantic search for her.

Aunt Sallie Pry had gone downstairs to the big kitchen to unpack the basket of food Dinah had sent. Being deaf, she could not hear what was going on. Therefore, it came as a tremendous surprise to her to be confronted suddenly by a strange gray kitten. The little animal, terrified in her new surroundings, leaped to a window sill, hoping perhaps to escape, but a screen prevented her from going outside.

"My goodness, where did you come from?" cried Aunt Sallie.

The Bobbsey twins heard her exclamation, and

knew that she had seen Smoky. They rushed to the kitchen and captured their pet.

"Flossie, you shouldn't have brought her," Nan scolded. "But since Smoky's here, she'll have to stay in the kitchen. We mustn't let her get into the rest of the house."

Flossie felt like crying. She had thought it would be such fun to surprise her brothers and sister, and play with the kitten at Mystery Mansion. It had not turned out that way at all!

Bert spied the covered basket which Dinah had sent, and suggested it as a place in which to keep Smoky. Flossie agreed, but said her pet must have something to eat first. She brought down the bag of food which she had hidden in her suitcase, and gave Smoky her supper, topped off with a saucer of milk. Then the kitten was put into the basket and the lid brought down far enough so that she could not get out.

After everyone had eaten supper the twins started to explore the strange house. They looked first at the chair that rocked all by itself. Now it was quite still. Corners in the house which had seemed dark and mysterious before seemed perfectly all right this evening. Even the queer-looking Chinese statues in the hall looked very picturesque.

"It's funny how we thought things were spooky when we were here before, isn't it?" Nan asked Bert. "There's not a thing mysterious—not even a—Oh!"

At that very instant there came a peculiar clicking sound from somewhere upstairs. What could it be?

Was it something they should investigate? Bert started up the stairway.

"Be careful!" Nan warned her brother.

Bert thought he knew what the noise might be. Upon reaching the second floor hall, the boy was sure he was right. Standing on a dresser in Sing Foo's bedroom was an unusual object which Bert assumed was a clock. On it were several figures which were jumping up and down.

The other children came into the room and gazed at the Chinese clock. Freddie and Flossie wanted to know how in the world one could tell time by it. The older twins confessed they had no idea.

"I suppose it's another one of Sing Foo's secrets," said Bert.

"Maybe he keeps the Golden Key inside of it," suggested Flossie.

Bert picked up the clock and looked inside. No key was concealed there.

"Let's get up early tomorrow and hunt for the Golden Key," suggested Freddie. "It's too dark now."

The others agreed, and decided that as soon after breakfast as they could finish helping Aunt Sallie with her work, they would start their search. By nine o'clock the guests at Mystery Mansion were in their beds and sound asleep. Shortly afterward Mrs. Pry put out the lights and retired.

About three hours later Nan awoke with a start. Somewhere far off she was sure she could hear a faint cry. The Bobbsey girl listened intently.

"Where can it be coming from?" she wondered. "Is it inside the house or out in the garden?"

Finally Nan got up, put on her robe and slippers and went out into the hall. The cry was from some place inside the house!

"I wonder what it can be!" she thought. "Maybe it's one of Sing Foo's secrets!"

The girl tiptoed to the bedroom where Bert and Freddie were sleeping and gently awakened her twin.

"Come with me," she said softly. "Something's wrong in the house."

Bert, instantly awake, scrambled into his own robe and slippers and followed his sister into the dark hall. A second later he too heard the sound.

"I'm sure it's downstairs," said the boy.

"Do you know how to turn on the lights?" Nan asked him.

"I think so," her twin replied.

In a moment Bert found a wall switch and flooded the upper hall with light. Together the Bobbseys walked to a back stairway. Now they could hear the cry very plainly.

"Oh, I know what it is," said Nan. "Smoky!"

"I guess you're right. She doesn't like staying alone."

There was no doubt that the kitten was scared. Her cries were not those of hunger; they were wails of fright.

The twins hurried down the stairway. They could not find the kitchen light, but it was not difficult to locate Smoky, because she was crying pitifully.

"I'll take her to my room," said Nan, and stooped down to get the basket from under the sink.

At this instant the two children heard a long, low whistle outside. As there were no houses near Mystery Mansion, they wondered who could be outside at this hour of the night.

"Maybe someone's coming here," said Nan fearfully.

"I don't hear the whistle now," Bert replied. Then suddenly he cried, "Look!"

Through a window the children could see moving lights some distance away. They drew nearer, and presently the twins heard the sound of a motor.

"It's a car," said Bert. "What is it doing on Sing Foo's property?"

Nan replied that perhaps there was a side road and someone was going home late. Two minutes afterward the car stopped. Its motor was turned off and the lights put out.

"Oh, Bert, do you think that means trouble here?" Nan asked.

The same answer crossed the minds of both children. Sing Foo's property was unguarded. Mystery Mansion was full of treasures. The occupants of the car might well be burglars!

"I'm going out and see what's doing," Bert announced, stepping to the kitchen door.

Nan ran over and held him back. "Please don't," she pleaded. "It's too dangerous. What could you do against a lot of thieves?"

CHAPTER XI

FREDDIE'S FIND

"WE ought to help Aunt Sallie guard Sing Foo's property," Bert Bobbsey told his twin sister. "If burglars are coming here to rob this place, I'm going to stop them!"

Nan argued that it would be much better to call the police.

"Mystery Mansion is so far out of town the police couldn't get here in time," Bert replied.

At this moment the children heard the low whistle again. Ten seconds later the car lights were turned on, the motor was started, and the automobile turned around. It went down the road in the same direction from which it had come, and soon the twins could no longer see it.

Nan wanted to go right upstairs, but Bert thought perhaps they should wait around for a while to see if anyone might break into the house.

"Maybe one of the thieves whistled to tell the other fellows it was all right to come here," he said.

Nan shivered when she heard this. "But, Bert, we couldn't do a thing," she insisted.

Her twin wondered about this himself. Finally

he answered that if they should make a great racket and turn on some of the lights, they might scare away any housebreakers.

"Let's do it!" said Nan. "I know where a radio is. We'll turn it on."

"I'll watch here," said Bert. "You go ahead."

Unfortunately the girl could not find a single light switch. After bumping into several pieces of furniture Nan gave up the idea of the radio. She returned to Bert, and together they stood on guard for half and hour. When nothing happened the twins concluded they must have been mistaken about thieves coming to Mystery Mansion.

"We'd better go back to bed," stated Nan.

She picked up the basket with Smoky inside, and started up the back stairs. Bert followed reluctantly. Though they both were tired, they were too excited to fall asleep immediately, and it was some little time before they dozed off.

The next morning when Aunt Sallie saw Nan come downstairs with Smoky in her basket, the woman inquired how the pet had got upstairs. Upon hearing the cat had cried during the night, Mrs. Pry remarked:

"I guess you'd better take her upstairs tonight also. I don't like having you children wander around alone in a dark house."

Bert appeared in the kitchen at this moment. He told his twin he was going outside to look for footprints.

"I'd like to know how close that man who whistled last night came to the house," he remarked.

Aunt Sallie asked what the boy was talking about. She guessed from the look on his face that something had happened. He pointed out the window.

"We saw a light last night," he said.

"You saw a kite at night!" Mrs. Pry exclaimed. "Why would anyone fly a kite at night?"

"Not a kite—a light!" Bert shouted. "Someone stopped near here in a car."

"You say someone dropped a light not far from here?" Aunt Sallie asked.

In a loud voice Bert repeated what he had said and added, "We heard a whistle, too."

When the elderly woman understood what he was saying she became very much concerned.

"I don't like the idea of people stopping here at night," she said. Then after a moment's thought she went on, "But maybe there was nothing to it. Perhaps the car expected to pick up someone who was walking across the fields and he whistled to let the driver know where he was."

In her own mind Aunt Sallie was not too sure about this, but she did not want to frighten the children, especially the small twins. Freddie and Flossie had come into the kitchen and were listening wide-eyed to Bert's story.

"I'll have to be a detective and find out about it," announced Freddie.

"Suppose you come with me and we'll look for footprints," suggested Bert.

Nan told them that breakfast was ready, and that

they had better wait until later for their detective work. Also, she reminded her brothers that they had come to help Aunt Sallie take care of the pets in Mystery Mansion.

"That's right," agreed Bert.

Willingly the children helped with the work. After breakfast Nan and Flossie washed the dishes and made the beds. Then they looked for Mrs. Pry and the boys, who by this time had finished feeding the tropical fish.

"You're just in time to help with the birds," Aunt Sallie announced. "I'll show you how to give them their baths."

Flossie asked if it was done the same way they gave their canary a bath at home. The woman smiled, saying no, and added, "Why, I'd never get through if I had to give each bird a bath separately."

"Sing Foo has his birds well trained," she told the twins, "and he lets them play with one another for a while each morning."

She directed the children to help her carry a dozen of the small cages into a warm, sunshiny room. From a closet she brought out a large shallow pan and filled it with water. After placing it on the floor, she asked the twins to step outside the room.

"You may look through the glass in the door and watch the birds," Aunt Sallie said.

After the children had gone outside, she closed the door carefully and locked it from within. Then one by one she opened the doors to the cages and the pretty birds, chirping their thanks, hopped out. Some of them flew around the room, while others went directly to the pan of water on the floor. First they took a drink, then boldly stepped into the water, splashing it about with their wings.

It was fun to watch the birds take their baths. No two did it alike. Some merely threw water over themselves with their bills. Others dipped their heads in. A few crouched down so that the water might cover their bodies. But they all dried themselves in the same manner: they ruffled up their feathers and shook themselves as hard as they could to throw off the water.

While the birds bathed, Mrs. Pry cleaned the cages and put fresh food in the cups. Then a most surprising thing happened. She tinkled a little bell which hung in a corner of the room, and immediately each bird flew back into its cage. Aunt Sallie opened the door and asked the Bobbseys to come in and help her carry the cages back where they belonged.

"Thank you so much," she said. "I really think you children have done enough work for one morning. Suppose you go and play. After I've finished here I'll take you over to the pagoda."

The children had almost forgotten about Sing Foo's pagoda. They wondered what it was like. While waiting for Aunt Sallie, Nan and Flossie thought they would look for the Golden Key. Bert and Freddie still wanted to hunt for footprints outdoors.

"I'll be right outside," Bert said to Nan. "If you find anything interesting upstairs, let me know."

Freddie already was in the yard. He had no particular plan of where to search for footprints, so he just ran here and there, gazing steadily at the ground. When Bert reached him, Freddie said he thought they ought to go out to the road.

"That's where the car was, didn't you say, Bert?"

His brother replied that the car had been on the road, but the person who whistled seemed to have been nearer the house. The two boys hunted intently for footprints close to the Mansion but could not find any. Finally Bert agreed to go out to the road.

"Oh, Bert, look!" cried Freddie suddenly.

In the dirt along the side of the narrow road lay a key. The little boy picked it up and showed it to his brother.

"Maybe this is the Golden Key," he called out excitedly.

Bert looked at the object. It was not a golden key; in fact, it was just an ordinary key, silver in color.

"What do you suppose it fits?" asked Freddie eagerly. "One of Sing Foo's secrets?"

"Maybe," Bert replied, although the boy hardly thought so.

While he did not tell Freddie, he was inclined to think that the man who had whistled the night before had dropped it. Maybe it fit one of the doors of Mystery Mansion, and the reason the man had not tried to come inside was because he had lost the key!

Freddie already was running toward the house,

planning to try the key on various outside doors. Bert followed, and the two boys sped from place to place. They went all around the house, but the key did not fit any of the outside doors to Mystery Mansion.

"Maybe it fits something inside the house," suggested Freddie. "Sing Foo might have dropped it when he was out on the road."

He and Bert went in and tried all the doors on the first floor of the Mansion. The key did not fit any of them. On the second floor they had no better luck. The brothers finally came to the conclusion that the key never had belonged to Sing Foo.

"Maybe you ought to put it back in the road where it was," said Bert. "The person who dropped the key may come back for it."

Before they had a chance to do this, Nan, Flossie and Mrs. Pry walked into the hall.

"I've finished my work now," said Aunt Sallie. "If you like, I'll take you all down to the pagoda."

Freddie was so interested in this he decided not to bother about the key any more and put it into his pocket. At last he and the other twins were going to see the Chinese building they had heard so much about! Eagerly they followed Mrs. Pry, who led them through a series of beautiful gardens.

The children had never seen anything like them. Here and there were pools of water with arched bridges over them. Elf-like statues were set beside beds of sweet-smelling flowers. Even the flowers themselves were new varieties to the twins.

"Oh, isn't this place lovely?" cried Nan.

Practical Bert wanted to know whether Sing Foo took care of the extensive grounds himself. Aunt Sallie said he did, mostly because he loved gardening.

"But how he does it all I don't know," she sighed. "I'd like to do some weeding for him, but I'm afraid I shouldn't know weeds from good plants."

"Oh, is that the paggody?" exclaimed Flossie suddenly, pointing ahead of her.

"You mean *pagoda*," laughed Nan.

As the twins hastened toward the unusual looking but attractive building, Mrs. Pry explained that really it was a little church. She said sometimes wealthy Chinese have pagodas on their estates.

"Have you ever been inside this one?" Nan asked.

"No, I haven't," Aunt Sallie replied. "But it must be very beautiful."

When they reached the pagoda, the children gazed at it for several minutes. The building was not large, but very picturesque. It was made of wood, painted red and gold, and had a sloping roof which extended in a graceful way out beyond the side walls. There seemed to be no windows, but the pagoda had a very attractive front door on which was carved a serpent.

Aunt Sallie tried to open the door. When it did not yield, Bert pushed his weight against it. Finding this would do no good he said it must be locked.

"Freddie, maybe that key you found fits this door," he suggested.

Quickly the small twin reached into his pocket. A queer look came over his face.

"What's the matter?" Nan asked him.

Freddie did not reply for a few moments. He put his hand into every pocket of his clothes. Finally he said with a tremor in his voice:

"I—I guess I've lost the key!"

CHAPTER XII

THE CHINESE DINNER

A HUNT was started for the missing key. The Bobbseys and Aunt Sallie Pry looked around the pagoda
and then went back through the gardens. It was not
until they got all the way to the house that they had
to admit defeat.

"Maybe it dropped into one of the pools," suggested Flossie.

"But I wasn't near them," declared Freddie.
"And there aren't any holes in my pockets. I don't
see how the key could have fallen out."

Nan was inclined to think her small brother had
laid the key down and forgotten about it, so a search
was made inside Mystery Mansion. But it was no-
where in sight.

"I guess we'll just have to forget it," sighed Nan.
"You know what I think?" she asked as an idea
came to her. "I'll bet that key wouldn't fit the pagoda anyway. It's too ordinary."

The others agreed. She suggested they forget it
and go on a further hunt for the Golden Key.

As the children ran off to search through Mystery
Mansion, Aunt Sallie sat down in a chair to rest and

think things over. She wondered why Sing Foo had not told her more about the pagoda. He had said nothing about a key to it, and she had got the impression the building was unlocked.

"But I don't see why he would have left it unlocked if it has beautiful things inside," she reflected.

Suddenly a disturbing thought came to her. Suppose the people who had stopped near by in the car the night before had taken things from the pagoda and then locked the door!

"Oh, I do wish we could get inside," she said to herself. "But, then, I don't know what good that would do either. Sing Foo never told me what was in the pagoda, so how would I know whether or not anything has been taken out?"

In the meantime the four Bobbsey twins were hurrying from room to room of the old Mansion looking for the Golden Key. Nearly half an hour went by when suddenly Bert gave a shout.

"Come here!" he cried out. "Nan! Flossie! Freddie! What do you know about this?"

His sisters and brother came running to a closet in the second floor hall. In a back corner of it Bert had made a discovery. Now he came toward the others, carrying a little teakwood box in his arms.

"Is the Golden Key in there?" asked Freddie.

"No," Bert answered. "But there's something else and it's for us."

"What do you mean?" Nan asked him eagerly.

For answer her twin opened the lid. Inside, on a large piece of paper, was written:

FOR THE BOBBSEY TWINS

"What is it?"

"Who wrote it?"

"Let me see!"

Bert laughed. "I don't even know myself what's here," he said.

The boy set the box down and took out the sheet of paper. Underneath it were several cans of food. One by one the children removed them and read the labels.

"A Chinese chow mein dinner!" exclaimed Nan delightedly.

"Is it much trouble to fix?" Flossie wanted to know. "I'd like to try it right away."

The twins trooped downstairs to find Aunt Sallie. When they showed her what Bert had found, the elderly woman laughed.

"Sing Foo told me he was going to hide some things around the house for you children. This must have been one of them," she said. "Shall we have the Chinese dinner this noon?"

"Oh, yes!" the twins cried together.

Flossie looked at Aunt Sallie. "May we sit on the floor and eat our chow mein with chopsticks?" she asked.

The little girl had noticed that at the bottom of the box there were several sets of chopsticks, so she was sure this was the way Sing Foo wanted them to eat the dinner.

Aunt Sallie did not understand the little girl's question, and thought when she said *chopsticks* that she was asking if the chow mein was like *chops,* and whether it would *stick* to the pan when she cooked it. Flossie tried hard not to giggle.

Everyone helped to get the meal ready. Bert opened the cans of food. Aunt Sallie steamed some rice, Chinese style, while Nan warmed up the chicken chow mein, the mushroom sprouts, and the soy bean sauce. Then she arranged almond cakes and rice wafers on a plate and opened a package of tea.

"Make the tea very weak," ordered Aunt Sallie. "Freddie and Flossie should have milk instead, but we want to have our Chinese dinner correct."

In the dining room Flossie had placed several pillows in a circle on the floor. Freddie had found a number of bowls in a closet, and placed them in front of the pillows. Then he put a set of chopsticks inside each bowl.

When the food was ready, Aunt Sallie and Nan carried it into the dining room. The elderly woman laughed when she saw the pillows.

"I guess I'm too old to sit on the floor," she said. "I believe I'll sit in this armchair beside you and eat my chow mein and cakes."

What a jolly dinner hour it turned out to be! At first the small twins did not think they were going to like the chow mein, but after a few mouthfuls they declared it to be very tasty. In the end, there was not a scrap of food left.

"Oh, I feel as if I'm going to burst," said Freddie, getting up.

The others laughed and said they all felt the same

way. The Chinese dinner had been a great success!

"Well, Sing Foo's first secret was pretty nice," declared Nan. "I wonder what else we'll find hidden."

"Let's hunt for more things," suggested Bert eagerly.

Although the search continued for a while, the Bobbsey children did not come across anything else. As a matter of fact, it was only Bert and Nan who continued to hunt. Flossie and Freddie had become so drowsy after their big meal that they had lain down and gone to sleep.

When it was time to feed the birds again, Aunt Sallie called to the older twins. Bert and Nan giggled. It seemed to them that between people, fish and birds, eating at Mystery Mansion was a continuous procedure!

"Aunt Sallie told me there are some rare birds here we haven't seen," stated Nan, as they went to help her. "I wonder if we'll see them now."

The girl asked Aunt Sallie about this. She nodded yes, and added that she had a special job for Bert.

"But first," the woman said, "I'll show you the parrots. I can't hear them talk, but Sing Foo thinks they are very interesting."

The parrots were not in separate cages. They lived together in a large room called an aviary. Each bird sat on a stout perch at the top of a pole, with a little chain fastened around its leg. The other end of the chain was attached to the pole.

"Are they friendly birds?" Nan asked Mrs. Pry.

"Yes indeed," the woman answered. "They've never bothered me."

Bert and Nan thought they had never seen a more beautiful sight. There were at least twenty-five parrots of different colors. Several of them were pure white. A few were blue, others were green and gold or green and yellow, and some had as many as six colors in their feathers.

As the twins entered the aviary, the various birds began to call out. None of them said the usual "Polly wants a cracker." They were very polite, and made remarks such as "How do you do, sir?" "Good afternoon, Miss. I'm glad you came."

A few said words the children could not understand, and they supposed these were in Chinese.

Aunt Sallie had gone to a little closet at the side of the room. Now she handed each of the twins a box of seed and told them to fill the feeding cups. While they did this the woman got some water and one by one gave the birds a drink.

The children were much amused at the response the parrots made to this. Several of them said "Thank you," and one of the old ones bobbed his head up and down, remarking, "Good afternoon. You needn't stay any longer."

In a few minutes Aunt Sallie led the way from the aviary and took the twins to another large room which they had not seen before. In the center of it was a big cage like those one finds in public zoos. Inside were several small trees. Fluttering among the branches or strutting around on the gravel floor were a number of large birds. Bert and Nan recognized a peacock, a stork, and a flamingo.

"Oh, aren't they wonderful!" exclaimed Nan excitedly.

"Yes, they're wonderful to look at," Aunt Sallie agreed, "but in many ways they are not so interesting as the smaller birds. Some of them are not friendly and once in a while they fight among themselves."

"Then why does Sing Foo put them together?" Bert asked.

"They need lots of space to stalk around in, and Sing Foo hasn't enough room here to separate them," the woman replied. "He said that anyway they don't thrive very well living alone."

Bert inquired how one took care of them if they were unfriendly. Aunt Sallie answered that this was the special job she had for him.

"There's a suit here you are to put on before entering the cage," she directed the boy.

From the closet she took a strange-looking outfit. It included a one-piece padded khaki suit, a helmet with heavy goggles, and long gauntlets.

Bert donned the costume. Then Aunt Sallie gave him a bucket of feed and one of water.

"Put them in those troughs, and then I'll hand you a rake," she said. "Scratch up the gravel with it."

As the boy entered the big cage the woman warned him to watch out for the birds. He should be perfectly safe from their claws or beaks, being so well covered; yet it would not hurt to be watchful of them. It was well that the Bobbsey boy had been told this, because the birds did not like the strange-looking object which came toward them. Several of them flew directly at Bert and tried to peck him.

Paying no attention to them, Bert filled the pans with food and water. The great birds shrieked, flapped their wings, and came to feed.

Bert now took the rake, which Aunt Sallie handed to him through the bars of the cage, and began scratching up the gravel. He did not notice that in passing a tree one of the branches brushed against his left gauntlet, turning the top of it down over his hand. Apparently a large, unfriendly heron spied this. Instantly it came winging toward the Bobbsey boy.

"Go away!" Bert cried in a muffled voice behind his helmet.

Before he could dodge, the heron sank his sharp bill into the lad's wrist.

Bert cried out in pain!

CHAPTER XIII

SURPRISE VISITORS

As BERT BOBBSEY fought off the big bird, he turned the cuff of his gauntlet up. The heron in anger, and perhaps frightened by the boy's cries, kept flying against him and pecking at his suit.

"Come out!" yelled Nan to her brother.

Bert needed no urging. He rushed to the door of the cage which Nan opened for him.

"Whew!" exclaimed Bert, pulling off his helmet. Perspiration was running down his face.

"Let me see your hand," said Nan.

Her twin pulled off his gauntlet. Blood was running from a wound on the boy's wrist. His sister took a handkerchief from her pocket and bandaged it. Then she helped him out of the padded suit.

"We'll put these clothes away later," she said. "I'd better fix your wrist first."

Together they sought Aunt Sallie, who had gone into the next room, and asked her where the antiseptic and bandages were. The elderly woman was concerned about Bert, and said she never should have let him go into the cage with the unfriendly birds.

"Oh, this isn't anything," the boy insisted.

"Nevertheless, Nan is right. We must put something on it," Mrs. Pry said firmly.

She led the way to a little closet where Sing Foo kept supplies. Deftly Nan bandaged her brother's wrist. Freddie and Flossie, who had awakened from their naps, came to see what had happened.

"Oo, I'm glad that bad bird didn't peck your eyes," remarked Flossie, after she had heard the story.

"So am I," agreed Bert. "The way that old fellow went after me was no fun."

After Aunt Sallie was sure the boy was all right, she said she was going to feed the tropical fish, and wouldn't Freddie and Flossie like to help her? The small twins were delighted and trotted down the basement stairs after the woman. She gave each of them a box of white wafers, telling them to break the food into small pieces and scatter it over the various pools and tanks.

The twins separated, since there were two rooms containing fish. Aunt Sallie went off to attend to something else, leaving Freddie and Flossie entirely alone. Freddie followed the woman's instructions about the wafers with all but one of them. Feeling slightly hungry, the little boy could not resist the temptation of biting into it.

"Not bad," he said to himself.

Sitting down at the edge of a pool, he slowly munched the wafer and watched the fish come to the surface of the water and nibble their supper. One

fish interested Freddie very much. He began to wonder why it was called a gold fish anyway; it was not
gold in color at all. It was black, and had large, bulb-
ous eyes, which looked like lanterns set in the front
of its head. The fish had a small tail that wiggled
back and forth swiftly.

"I should think the tail would get tired," thought
Freddie.

There was a red and white fish which made the
little boy laugh. In his mind he nicknamed it the somersault fish because it did not swim in a straight line;
instead, it continuously made loops in the water. The
funny fish would come to the surface to take a bite
of food, and then dive down and turn another somersault.

In the other room Flossie was having a little adventure of her own. Worried because some of the
larger fish seemed to be getting all the food, she got
a little stick, which was standing in a corner, and
tried to move the pieces of wafer around on the top
of the water.

"Go away, you greedy old thing," she said aloud
to a black and white polka dot specimen. "Let the
little fish have some."

Three small fish were trying to get bites from the
wafer, but the larger fish kept shoving them out of
the way. Flossie decided to do something about this.
Reaching far over, she gently pushed the polka dot
fish aside with her stick.

In her eagerness the little girl did not realize she
was reaching too far. The next instant she lost her

balance, waving her arms wildly to save herself.

"Oh!" she screamed, then plop! and Flossie Bobbsey was in the water.

In the next room her twin heard the cry. Jumping up, Freddie rushed out to see what the trouble was. His sister was just coming to the surface of the pool.

"Flossie!" cried the little boy in fright.

He did not know how deep the water was. Also he wondered if his twin would remember how to swim. But the little girl did not lose her head. Though she did not swim very well, Flossie could keep herself afloat. Fortunately she was not many feet from the edge of the pool and quickly splashed to the edge.

Freddie leaned down and helped her out of the water. He asked how she happened to fall in.

"I was trying to push a greedy fish out of the way," the little girl explained. "What's the matter?" she asked, as she noticed how intently Freddie was looking at her.

Flossie was a sight. Water was running from her clothes and her hair. She had pieces of loose seaweed and fish wafers all over her dress.

"You'd better change your clothes," Freddie suggested.

His sister thought so too, and started from the room. In the hall outside she met Aunt Sallie, who looked at the child in amazement.

"Flossie Bobbsey, whatever in the world have you been doing?" she cried.

Freddie explained for his twin, while the little girl went on to her bedroom. Getting clean after her dip in the pond was not so simple as Flossie had thought. Aunt Sallie, who had followed her upstairs, insisted that the little girl have a tub bath and a shampoo.

"If you don't, you'll certainly have the odor of fish on you," the woman told her, "and I don't think you'd like that."

Flossie, spic and span again, barely had finished telling her story to Bert and Nan, when the children heard a car outside. Running to see who had come, they were delighted to discover the callers were Mr. and Mrs. Bobbsey.

"Daddy! Mother!" they all exclaimed at once.

"You haven't come to take us home, have you?" asked Freddie fearfully.

His parents smiled, and assured their small son that they had no intention of doing this.

"We just wanted to be sure you're all right and having a good time," said Mrs. Bobbsey.

The twins said they were, and eagerly told of their various adventures at Mystery Mansion.

"My goodness!" laughed Mr. Bobbsey. "You've had enough excitement for a whole week. I wonder if I can remember what you've just told me. Let's see—Flossie fell in the pond, Bert got pecked on the wrist, Nan had to take care of poor, frightened Smoky, Freddie lost a key, and—"

"And don't forget we went to see the paggody," said Flossie.

Nan explained to her father that Flossie meant the pagoda. She remarked that they still hoped to get inside the building.

"There are lots of mysteries around here," said Flossie. "We found one."

"What was that?" her mother asked.

Her small daughter explained about the teak-wood box holding the chow mein dinner, and how Sing Foo had hidden it. Bert told his parents about the strange whistling he and Nan had heard the night before, and of how the mysterious car had stopped on the road for a short time.

"We thought maybe thieves were in it," the boy said. "Perhaps they took things out of the pagoda."

Mr. Bobbsey inquired how long the car had been parked, and whether they were sure it was a car.

"It might have been a truck," he said.

"It didn't sound like a truck," said Bert. "And it didn't stay here very long."

"Long enough to change a flat tire?" asked Mr. Bobbsey.

Bert and Nan said they hardly thought so. When their father heard this he remarked that if there had been thieves in the car, they could not have removed very many things from the pagoda in such a short while.

"However, they could have taken some small and very valuable things," Mr. Bobbsey said. "I believe I'll write to Sing Foo and tell him about this."

Mrs. Bobbsey asked her husband whether he thought it would be safe to leave the children at Mystery Mansion another night. She did not like the idea of strangers prowling around near by. The children's father doubted that there was any danger.

"If there had been burglars around they certainly would have come into the house," he said, and added he was sure it would be all right for the twins to stay at Mystery Mansion, especially since they had watchmen.

"Watchmen?" Bert asked.

"Certain birds are very good watchmen," his father replied. "I believe if any stranger were to break into the Mansion at night, some of the birds in the basement would sense it and set up a great noise."

The four children showed Mr. and Mrs. Bobbsey around the house. Then, when they were ready to leave, Bert said quietly to his father:

"Have you heard anything more about the counterfeit money?"

Mr. Bobbsey looked serious. "I'm sorry I haven't a better report for you, son," he replied. "But that story about my passing bad money has been told all over town. Everywhere I go someone asks me about it, and when I buy anything, it's very embarrassing the way people look intently at the money I hand them."

Bert was furious to hear this. He still thought that Danny Rugg was back of the whole thing. He could not prove it, of course, but he intended to investigate further as soon as he should get home.

"That bully just isn't going to get away with it!" the Bobbsey boy said emphatically.

Mr. Bobbsey laid a hand on Bert's shoulder. He thanked him for his loyalty, but advised his son to be careful of what he said to Danny Rugg.

"People can get into a great deal of trouble making false accusations," he stated.

The boy promised, but determined to find out all he could as soon as possible. If the bully were guilty, Bert was going to make him apologize to Mr. Bobbsey, and tell the other people in town that there was no truth in the story about the Bobbsey family trying to pass counterfeit money.

"In a way, I hope it was Danny," said Bert's father, as he got ready to drive off from Mystery Mansion. "That would not be so serious for me as if a grown-up had said it."

Bert was glad his father felt this way about the matter, but the boy thought that regardless of who had said it, the story was a dreadful thing. And he was not going to let the matter rest. He would find out the truth!

CHAPTER XIV

THE STATUE THAT TALKED

AFTER Mr. and Mrs. Bobbsey had gone, the children went back inside the Mansion. Nan found Aunt Sallie dusting and offered to help her. The elderly woman got another cloth and gave it to the girl.

"Suppose you dust that room where Sing Foo put on his show the first time you were here," Mrs. Pry suggested.

"All right," agreed Nan. "But I guess I won't touch the chair that rocks by itself."

The room was somewhat dark but Nan thought she would be able to do her work without turning on a light. The girl knew there were a great many small objects in the room, but she did not realize how many there were until she began picking them up, one by one, to dust them.

"Oh, isn't this adorable?" Nan said suddenly, half aloud.

On a table, arranged in a ring, was a complete set of beautifully carved wild animals. They were very tiny, and the girl wondered how the sculptor had made them so perfect. Near them stood two white horses about three inches long. Standing on the back of each horse was a dainty girl in a fancy riding costume.

"Circus bareback riders," thought Nan. "Oh, and here are some more things from a circus."

In a glass case was a miniature trapeze with tiny figures on it; some were sitting on the bars, and others hung in mid-air. Nan could not see the tiny wires which held these in place, and it looked to her as if the figures actually were flying through space.

"They're wonderful," she thought.

The girl suddenly realized she was doing more looking than dusting, and decided she had better get to work. For several minutes she carefully wiped specks of dirt from table tops and ornaments. Coming to a corner of the room, Nan gazed in awe at a beautiful green-colored statue which she had not noticed before. It was a life-size half-figure of a man with one arm slightly upraised.

The Bobbsey girl began to dust the figure rather vigorously. Suddenly she drew back in fright. The head had begun to nod at her!

"Oh!" she cried.

An instant later, however, the girl smiled. The head of the statue must be meant to move, she thought. Again she applied the cloth to the figure. No sooner had she done this than the man began to raise his right arm.

This time Nan stepped some distance away from the statue. She found herself trembling a little at the strange sight.

"Perhaps I'd better go," Nan thought, but in-

stantly reflected that she did not want her brothers
and sister to think a statue had scared her.

As she stood still, staring, the man began to
speak. Nan did not know what he was saying, because he spoke in Chinese, but there was no doubt
that he was talking. His lips had parted, his head
was turning from side to side, and now his other arm
was rising.

"Oh, he's a real man!" Nan quavered.

It suddenly occurred to her that someone had hidden in a dark corner of the room and was pretending
to be a statue. In terror she fled to the hall, slam-
ming the door behind her and calling loudly for Bert.

Her twin dashed down the stairs, demanding to
know what the trouble was. Nan was so frightened
she could hardly speak. Finally she managed to gasp
out what had occurred in the strange room.

"Maybe—maybe the burglar got in here after
all," she said.

Aunt Sallie Pry, who had finished her dusting in
another part of the house, came into the hall and
saw the look of fright on Nan's face. Quickly Bert
explained what had happened and said he was going
to investigate.

"You'll do nothing of the sort," said Mrs. Pry. "I
shall go first."

She opened the door to the strange room, snapped
on a light, and walked toward the statue. Bert and
Nan, close at her heels, gazed at the object. The boy
was a bit surprised his twin had thought the figure
might be real.

"It's only a statue," he told her.

Seeing the green-colored statue standing perfectly still now made Nan feel very much embarrassed. She blushed and remarked that it certainly was anything but human.

"Show us what you did to the statue," Bert suggested.

Nan stepped up and touched the man's head with her dust cloth. Almost at once it began to nod at the three of them. In a few seconds one arm of the figure began to rise. A moment later the head turned from side to side, the lips parted, and the strange words issued from its mouth. Then the other arm lifted.

As the three stared at it, the statue ceased speaking, the lips closed, the head returned to its normal position, and the arms went down into place once more.

"Nan, you touched something to make it work," cried Bert, dashing forward. "I'm going to find out what it is."

"Be careful," warned Aunt Sallie. "Don't get your fingers pinched."

The Bobbsey boy touched the statue's head the way Nan had. As it went through its queer performance again, he listened carefully. Bert was sure he could hear a clicking noise inside the figure.

"I'll bet there's a record inside of it," he decided.

He tried to lift up the statue, but it was too heavy. He asked Nan to help him, and together the twins tilted the figure on the pedestal. Bert had been right in his guess. Beneath the hollow statue was a minia-

ture phonograph with a tiny record on it. A wire attached to a little lever ran up to the neck of the man.

Inside the figure were several other wires, and the
twins supposed these controlled the arms and head.
After they had set the man back in place, Bert remarked:

"I'm going to try it again."

He touched the head, but this time nothing happened.

"Oh, my goodness, we've broken it!" cried Nan.

Aunt Sallie was worried. She felt responsible for
anything the twins might do during their stay with
her. She declared they ought to fix the wires at once
if they possibly could do so.

"I'll try," said Bert.

For half an hour Nan, Aunt Sallie and Bert attached first this wire, then that; unfastened this one,
then another. Finally they got everything to work
except the little record which spoke the Chinese
words.

"I guess we'll have to let that go," sighed Aunt
Sallie. "I must see about supper now."

After she had gone off, Bert and Nan remained in
the strange room. They tried for several more minutes to make the mechanism work correctly.

"If I could only see better what's inside the statue,
I believe I might fix it," said the boy.

"I know where there's a flashlight," Nan offered,
and ran to get it.

With the aid of this, Bert presently found a lever
which evidently had been turned off by mistake.

When he moved it over to another position, the little record began to play.

"Thank goodness," the lad said in relief. "Now we'll see if everything works in the right order."

He put the statue firmly on the pedestal and touched the head. This time it went through all the motions in the correct sequence. More light-hearted than they had been for half an hour, the twins grinned at each other. Nan thought that Freddie and Flossie would like to watch the man perform, so she walked into the hall and called them. When they did not reply, she went to the second floor and looked in the bedrooms. The twins were not in sight.

"They must have gone outdoors," Nan decided, and asked Bert to look for them.

But though the boy walked through all the gardens as far as the pagoda, calling to them, Freddie and Flossie did not answer. It was not until he returned, and Nan had searched more thoroughly through the house, that the older children became alarmed.

"What could have happened to them?" asked Nan fearfully.

CHAPTER XV

ABOUT the time Nan started to dust the strange statue, her small brother and sister, who had been exploring upstairs, found a door on the second floor which at first seemed to be locked. By tugging on it, the two of them got it open and saw a stairway leading to the attic of the big house. Closing the door behind them, they started up.

The place above was in total darkness, but after feeling around the wall Freddie found an electric switch, which snapped on a dim light. As the children reached the top step, they stood still and exclaimed in wonder.

"Oh!" cried Flossie. "There must be just millions of toys here!"

"I wonder if they're any good," remarked Freddie, gazing about. The little boy had noticed that things were piled up in disorder, and he thought it might be because they were in need of repair.

Flossie had picked up a small musical instrument. She could not remember the name of it, which was xylophone, but the little girl knew how it was played. She looked around for the little cloth-covered stick

115

with which to strike the pieces of metal and make notes ring out. In a moment she spied what she was searching for, and struck the xylophone.

Bong!

"Oh, let me see it!" cried Freddie.

Flossie did not know how to play a tune, but she struck the bars, making sweet musical sounds.

"Let's take it downstairs," she said, "and show it to Bert and Nan."

"Don't go yet," Freddie begged. "I see something!"

The little boy had spied an animal's head sticking up among the various toys.

"It looks like a horse but it's not a horse," he said, climbing over to reach the animal.

"Oh, I know what it is," cried Flossie. "It's—it's a baby zebra!"

"That's right," agreed Freddie. "I wonder what Sing Foo used it for."

The black and white striped animal was made of wood and was in good condition. As Freddie pulled it from the pile, he was amazed to find a rather long metal pole attached to the under side of its body.

"What do you suppose that's for?" he said.

Both children were sure they had seen something like it before, but they could not remember where. The answer did not come to them until a few minutes later, when Flossie discovered a small wooden lion which also had a pole attached to the under side of its body. Then she cried out:

"The animals are from a merry-go-round! Oh, I wish we could find it all and make it go."

Eagerly the twins searched among the piles of toys in the attic. One by one they unearthed an elephant, a tiger, and a giraffe. Unfortunately the giraffe was without a head.

"We can't make these work unless we find the floor to the merry-go-round," said Freddie.

The children searched for a long time but the floor did not seem to be anywhere around. Discouraged and somewhat tired, they sat down for several minutes and said nothing. It was very quiet in the attic.

Suddenly Flossie noticed something and grabbed Freddie's hand. In a dark corner were two glowing balls of fire! They moved slowly toward the startled twins.

Too frightened to stir, Freddie and Flossie clung together. Then from somewhere there came a slight noise. It sounded like Prrr-prrr. The twins were sure now that the eyes belonged to an animal.

Had one of the toys come to life?

Then an instant later the two children sighed in relief and laughed. An animal *was* walking toward them, but it was not one of the toys.

"Smoky!" cried Flossie. "Oh, you naughty kitten! You scared us! How did you get here?"

They knew she had not followed them, so there must be another entrance to the attic. Flossie picked up their pet and stroked her gently. The fuzzy kit ten rubbed her nose against the small girl's neck and purred contentedly.

Freddie, now that he knew there was nothing to be frightened about, got up and began searching again for the floor of the merry-go-round. Suddenly he laughed, and told his sister they were sitting right on it.

Putting down the kitten, Flossie helped her twin take everything off the merry-go-round base. Then, one by one, they stuck the wooden animals in the holes. Freddie gave the floor a twirl and they went round and round.

"Oh; isn't this fun!" Flossie exclaimed. "But we should have some music."

Freddie stopped the merry-go-round and climbed onto the zebra's back. Flossie seated herself on the tiger.

Unfortunately there was no one to make the merry-go-round go round, so finally Flossie climbed down and said Freddie might ride first. She brought over the xylophone, and while she used one hand to tap it, she turned the merry-go-round with the other.

Freddie thought this was wonderful. He asked his twin if she could make him go faster, but the little girl was doing her best as it was. In a few minutes her arms began to ache, so she stopped. Freddie had been having such a good time he had forgotten to give his sister a ride, but now he jumped down, saying he would turn the merry-go-round and bang the xylophone.

Flossie got on the tiger again and started her ride.

The toy did not go fast enough to suit Freddie, so he laid down the mallet with which he had been striking the xylophone, and used both his hands on the merry-go-round floor.

"Oh, don't go so fast!" begged Flossie.

But Freddie paid no attention. He wanted to see just how speedily he could twirl the little merry-go-round. Faster and faster Flossie was whirled.

"Stop!" she cried, clinging more tightly than ever to the tiger's head.

Still her twin refused to listen. Unfortunately, the animal on which Flossie was riding had not been fastened securely. Before the children knew what was happening, the tiger became loosened. The little girl and the wooden animal were flung off.

"Oh, Flossie!" cried her twin, fearful that he had hurt his sister.

Scampering over to her, the little boy helped Flossie to her feet. As it turned out, she was more frightened than anything else. Her leg hurt a little, she said, but she guessed she was all right.

"I'm terrible sorry," Freddie told her contritely. "Maybe we'd better not play any more."

His sister agreed. They were about to go downstairs when Flossie suddenly remembered Smoky.

"Where did she go?" the little girl asked.

Freddie admitted that he had not noticed. He felt that they should find the kitten, though, and take her downstairs. The little boy called her name.

Smoky did not come, so the children crawled all over the attic looking for her. At the far end was a door which was open just enough for a kitten to squeeze through.

"I'll bet Smoky went out this way," said Freddie.

He pushed the door wide open and found himself in a little room with a skylight in the ceiling. It was slightly ajar.

"Oh!" the little boy gasped.

At the top of a ladder which led to the skylight was the missing kitten.

"Smoky's going up to the roof!" he cried. "We must stop her!"

He called to the kitten, but instead of coming back, Smoky crawled through the open skylight to the roof of Mystery Mansion. At once Freddie climbed after her. As the little boy disappeared, Flossie decided to follow him.

When the twins reached the roof, Smoky was not in sight. They could not imagine where she had gone.

The roof on which the children were standing was flat, but Mystery Mansion was large and had many other sections of roof, some of which went up at a sharp angle. Flossie remarked that no doubt the kitten was on one of them.

"But I don't see her!" the little girl said.

"Look!" cried Freddie suddenly. "There's our Smoky!"

He pointed to their pet who was on top one of the peaked roofs near a large chimney. One side of the chimney had little steps. The kitten scooted up them, sat down on the rim, and looked inside. Spying her, Flossie cried out:

"Smoky! You come back here! You might fall in!"

The kitten turned around but did not obey her mistress. Freddie, wanting to be of help, stomped up and down, first on one foot, then the other, calling to her. This merely frightened the little animal.

Suddenly, as the children gazed at her, Smoky lost her balance and disappeared down the chimney!

CHAPTER XVI

THE SEARCH FOR SMOKY

FLOSSIE screamed. Freddie shouted. Then both children became silent as they stared at the chimney on top of Mystery Mansion. Finally Flossie said:

"Wh-where do you suppose Smoky went? I m-mean, how far down the chimney?"

Freddie could only guess. He, as well as his twin, had hoped to see the head of the little gray kitten come bobbing up over the top of the chimney. But after several minutes went by and this did not happen, they knew she must have fallen far down and could not get out.

"We'd better do something," stated the little boy.

Flossie wondered what they could do. Certainly it was impossible for them to climb over to the roof where the chimney was. She thought maybe Bert could do this, since he was bigger.

"Let's ask him," she said.

The small twins hurried to the skylight. As they were about to descend the ladder to the attic floor they heard their names called.

"Here we are!" said Flossie. "And something dreadful has happened!"

Nan and Bert came running toward the ladder. It was a relief to know the small children were safe. They had not heard Flossie's remark and inquired why their brother and sister were on the roof.

"It's dangerous. Don't ever do that again!" Nan scolded.

"Please do something!" said Flossie, paying no attention to her sister's words. "Bert, come up here and see if you can get Smoky out!"

"Whatever are you talking about?" asked Nan.

It took a few seconds to make the older twins understand that the kitten had fallen down the chimney, but the instant they realized it, the two of them dashed up to the roof.

"Smoky went down that chimney," explained Freddie, pointing. "Bert, maybe you can climb over there and get her out."

Nan was not sure her twin should attempt to do such a dangerous thing. The boy would have to scale a sharp, peaked section of roof in order to reach the chimney.

"Even if you could get there, maybe you couldn't get Smoky out," she stated.

"But we have to rescue her!" cried Flossie, tears rolling down her cheeks. "We can't ju-just let Smoky die in the chimney!"

"I know that," said Nan. "But we don't want Bert to lose his life, either."

The four children talked over the matter. Finally it was decided that they had better speak to Mrs. Pry before doing anything. When the woman heard what had happened, she went to the roof at once.

Bert in the meantime had been looking for some long pieces of rope. Finding two in the garage, he carried them upstairs, and said he had figured out how to rescue Smoky. Making a loop at the end of one rope, he swung it several times toward the chimney until he finally lassoed it. Then, with the help of Nan and Aunt Sallie, Bert tied the opposite end of the rope about his waist.

Carrying the other rope over his shoulders, the boy stepped across to the peaked roof and began pulling himself up, hand over hand, by the piece attached to the chimney. There was a small level space at the foot of the chimney itself, so when Bert reached this he was safe enough.

Quickly he climbed up the steps leading to the top of the chimney and looked down into the black, yawning hole. The lad could see nothing, but he could hear the pitiful cries of the little kitten.

"She's alive, anyway," Bert thought thankfully. "Now, if only I can get her out!"

He took the loose rope from his shoulders and let it dangle down the chimney, holding it much as a fisherman might while waiting for a tug on a line. Once he thought Smoky grabbed at the rope and slowly he pulled it upward. But suddenly the tension lessened, and the boy knew that either the kitten had fallen off, or the rope had caught on one of the bricks.

Again Bert let the rope down, this time all the way to the end. He felt sure it must have reached the bottom of the chimney, but Smoky did not grab it. She just cried piteously.

A dreadful thought came to the Bobbsey boy—perhaps poor Smoky was wedged between some bricks and could not get out! Discouraged, he turned to the group who were waiting on the other roof.

"I can hear the kitten but she doesn't grab hold of the rope," he said.

"Oh, please try again," urged Flossie.

Bert did as he was directed, but after several attempts he came to the conclusion that if the cat were to be rescued it would not be by this means. Slowly the Bobbsey boy climbed down the outside of the chimney, slid along the roof, and returned to the others.

"Oh, what are we going to do?" said Flossie. "Poor Smoky! I'll bet she's awful scared!"

Mrs. Pry had a suggestion. It was possible they could reach the kitten from one of the fireplaces, or else through a flue leading from the furnace.

The children thought this a good idea and scampered down the ladder to the attic. Hurrying from one fireplace to another in the house, they listened intently for Smoky's cry but they could not hear it.

"I'll go down the cellar and see about the furnace flue," offered Bert.

The rest trooped after him, but at this spot they had no better luck. Aunt Sallie and the boy even lifted out a pipe, but the kitten did not appear.

"Is there any other place we can look?" Bert asked Aunt Sallie.

"I don't know of any. But this house has so many odd things in it, maybe there's some other spot where the chimney comes down."

The Bobbseys hunted everywhere, but could find none. Finally Aunt Sallie told them to give it up and come have their supper, but the children felt too sad and worried to do this. It was not until the woman assured them the cat would be rescued somehow that they consented to eat. In the midst of the meal Bert suddenly banged his fist on the table, announcing that he had the solution.

"What is it?" the others cried eagerly.

"Call the fire department," he replied. "The chief helped us out when we had the dog fight, so maybe he'll send some men to rescue our cat. They have long ladders. They might put one inside the chimney and go down for Smoky."

The others thought this a splendid idea, and insisted that Bert go to the telephone at once and call up the Lakeport Fire Headquarters. After the Bobbsey boy explained what had happened at Mystery Mansion, the chief, who had answered the telephone, said he would send some men right out and see what they could do.

Freddie, who from the time he was a tiny child, had loved fires and fire engines, was in a state of high delight. But the little boy was a bit disappointed when the hook and ladder arrived without any excitement. He loved it when the engines came clanging up the street, sirens shrieking. Now the driver merely turned quietly into the grounds of

Mystery Mansion and stopped without so much as the toot of a horn.

Recognizing the Bobbsey children, he laughed, and asked if they never had a fire when they telephoned the department? Or were the men always going to be called to rescue animals?

"I understand this time it's a cat," he said.

Two other firemen, whom the twins had never seen before, jumped from the rear of the hook and ladder. One, who was the tallest man they had ever seen outside of a circus, was named John. He asked to be told the story of the missing Smoky in more detail.

"You say she fell down the chimney?" he remarked, after hearing it. "Well, we'll see what we can do. About how wide is the chimney inside, Bert?"

"I believe you could put a ladder in and climb down," said the Bobbsey boy.

"Humph!" remarked the giant fireman. "A pretty dirty job. Well, Bill," he called to the driver, "let's get started. Bring those lanterns and that short extension ladder."

It was dusk now, and the twins thought the men would have a hard time working on the roof in the dark. But suddenly Bill turned day into night. He swung one of the powerful searchlights on the hook and ladder toward the roof and every object stood out as clearly as in the daylight.

Bert led the way to the attic. Then when they reached the roof, he pointed out the rope he had used to pull himself up to the chimney. The Bobbsey boy felt very proud when the firemen praised this method of getting there.

"It was the only sensible way to get to the chimney," John stated. "I'll go up that way myself."

While he was pulling himself up, hand over hand, the two other firemen laid the long extension ladder from the flat roof to the chimney. One of them ran up it.

He and John looked into the chimney and decided one of them might try going down. The ladder was inserted, and the tall fireman began to descend.

Nan, the small twins, and Mrs. Pry had come up to the roof to watch. Their hearts were beating excitedly. Could John rescue Smoky?

"Any luck?" the other fireman called down the chimney.

The children could not hear the tall fireman's reply, but they would have been discouraged if they had. John had gone down as far as he could squeeze his body, but he had not found the kitten.

"I can hear the little thing crying," he stated.

John played his flashlight downward but he could not see Smoky.

"The cat must be wedged in between the bricks," he called up. "Hand me a rope."

The fireman above let one down, hoping Smoky would catch hold of it. But she did not do this, and at last the men were forced to give up.

It was not until John reappeared on the roof that the Bobbsey twins heard the worst. Sadly the group walked down to the first floor of Mystery Mansion.

"Isn't there anything we can do?" Nan pleaded with the firemen. "It seems just dreadful to leave the poor kitten in there to die."

The men looked at one another. Then John spoke up, "Yes, there's just one more thing we can do. Tear out the chimney."

"What do you mean?" asked Nan.

Before replying, John went off to look around the house. When he reached the kitchen, he gazed at the wall, then thumped on it. From most of the wall there came a hollow sound, but in one part his knocking produced a dull thud.

"The chimney comes down here," he said. "I'm inclined to think we'll find your kitten just behind this spot."

"Would you have to make a very big hole?" Nan asked him.

John replied this would depend on just where Smoky might be. He asked Mrs. Pry's permission to hack at the wall. The elderly woman did not know what to say. She wondered how Sing Foo would feel about such a procedure; on the other hand, she did not want to be responsible for the kitten losing its life.

"Go ahead," she said finally to the giant John.

The fireman warned her that the job would cause a lot of dirt, and suggested that she put things away and spread newspapers on the floor. The children helped her do this; that is, all the children except Flossie. The poor little girl was so fearful of another failure to rescue Smoky that she had left the scene and gone out-of-doors. The child felt like crying and did not want the firemen to see her.

The big searchlight was still turned on. It lit up the whole side of the house and the garden. As Flossie looked around, she thought she was alone, but suddenly the little girl became aware of a figure standing back of the hook and ladder.

"Come here!" a voice said to her.

Thinking the man who had spoken must be the nice driver named Bill, Flossie hurried around where he was. To her amazement the person who had called her was a total stranger.

"What's going on here?" the man demanded.

"Oh!" cried Flossie. "I thought I knew you."

"Never mind about that," said the man. "I said, what's going on here?"

The little girl started to back away, but the stranger caught her hand. "I'm not going to hurt you," he said, "but I want to know why this hook and ladder is here."

"To—to rescue our cat," Flossie replied fearfully. "Now let me go!"

"Not yet," said the man. "I want to know more about it. Who are you? And whose cat are you talking about?"

Flossie told the man the Bobbsey twins were staying with Aunt Sallie Pry for the week end to help her with the work. She also remarked this was because Sing Foo had gone away, and Aunt Sallie had a lot to do taking care of the birds and fish.

"Now, please let me go!" Flossie cried, on the verge of tears.

"Just a minute," said the man.

He asked the little girl several more questions about what was going on inside the Mansion. Now Flossie, though she was very young, knew enough not to tell him that there were treasures in the house. He was such a mean person he could well be a thief!

With a jerk she pulled away from him, ran around the side of the hook and ladder, and flew into the house. Instantly she sought out Bert to tell him what had happened. Bert rushed from Mystery Mansion at once and looked all around, but the stranger had vanished.

Carefully locking the front door, the two children returned to the kitchen to watch the progress of Smoky's rescue. The firemen had hacked out a good-sized hole in the wall, and black soot lay in piles on the floor.

"Did you find her?" asked Flossie eagerly.

"Not yet," Nan replied.

At this moment the giant fireman John stuck his head into the opening they had made in the chimney and called Smoky's name. The kitten gave no answering cry. The man played his flashlight around the interior. Then he announced that the passageway had been blocked off, and he would have to hack a little further inside the chimney.

John was so tall that Freddie found he could look into the opening right between the man's legs. Abruptly the small twin squeezed beneath him and stood up inside the chimney. At this very second Tom's pick hit the brick wall. A great shower of soot came down, covering Freddie Bobbsey completely. The little boy sputtered and choked.

"Ugh!" he cried, crawling out beneath the giant fireman's legs.

What a sight Freddie was!

Although everyone was worried about the rescue of the kitten, they had to burst into laughter at the little boy's appearance. He was black from head to foot.

"Daddy ought to see his Little Fireman now," said Nan. "He'd call you his Little Black Fireman!"

She tried to lead her small brother away to help him wash, but he would not go. It was bad enough being all dirty, but Freddie was not going to miss seeing the rescue of Smoky, no matter what happened.

Suddenly John gave a muffled exclamation inside the chimney. He mumbled something about a cat, and the next moment reached his long arm into the kitchen and presented the children with their lost pet.

"Smoky!" they all cried.

Poor Smoky looked as bad as Freddie. Her gray fur was filled with soot and her little white whiskers were coal black. But this fact made no difference to the twins. They were too much relieved to see the kitten. They thanked John and the other fireman over and over again for rescuing her.

When the excitement died down, Mrs. Pry asked

the men what should be done about the chimney. They told her it would be necessary to get a mason to cement it up. In the meantime, they would tack a board over the opening so no more soot could drop into the kitchen.

The kindly firemen drove off in a little while. Freddie was given a thorough scrubbing by Bert and put into his night clothes. Smoky tried to lick herself clean, but Nan and Flossie would not let her do this. They got damp cloths and wiped her until her fur once more was gray and her little whiskers snowy white.

Bert came downstairs in time to help Aunt Sallie clean up the kitchen. They had just finished this when the telephone rang.

"I'll answer it," the boy offered.

Going to the hall, he picked up the receiver and said "Hello." He had half expected to hear either his father's or his mother's voice. Therefore, it was a great surprise to him when someone said gruffly:

"I want all of you to get out of Sing Foo's house at once!"

"Who's speaking?" asked Bert.

"Never mind. I said, 'All of you get out of that house right away!'"

CHAPTER XVII

THE CHASE

BERT BOBBSEY's hands trembled with excitement as he held the telephone receiver. The strange man's words both worried and angered him.

"Who are you?" the boy demanded.

There was a slight pause; then the stranger replied he was the person who had bought Sing Foo's mansion.

"Bought it!" cried Bert. "Sing Foo didn't tell us anyone had bought it."

"I'm not going to argue with you," the gruff man stated. "I don't want anybody inside that house. It's mine, and I can do what I please with it. Now all of you get out of there at once or there'll be trouble!"

Bert reminded the man that there were birds and fish to be fed, and if everyone should leave the house, who would do this? The boy's question seemed to stump the man for a moment. Then he replied that someone would take care of this matter.

"Well, are you going to get out?" he asked insistently.

"We can't go tonight," stated Bert.

"Why not?" the stranger questioned.

The boy did not answer, but he made up his mind they were not going to move out unless Sing Foo told them to.

"You are to do as I say," the man shouted into the telephone. "And no back talk. Tell that deaf old lady to get out of there and take you kids with her. If you don't, you'll be sorry!"

There was a click at the other end of the line. Bert knew the demanding stranger had cut off the connection. The boy did not move for several seconds. Then he hung up the receiver and went to look for Nan.

His twin was very much worried when she heard about the conversation. She said no doubt they should tell Mrs. Pry.

"And maybe we ought to call up Mother and Daddy," she suggested.

Bert agreed this might be the best thing to do, so they telephoned to the Bobbsey house. Good old Dinah answered.

"Well, if it ain't de chilluns!" she exclaimed. "I'se right sorry, but yo' folks is out fo' de evening. Kin I give dem a message when dey comes in?"

"Oh, never mind, Dinah," said Bert. "We'll see them tomorrow, anyway."

The twins decided not to tell Mrs. Pry about the stranger after all. She would only worry.

"Do you think he may try to break in here tonight?" asked Nan fearfully.

Bert said he hoped not. In any case, he was going to be sure all the windows and doors were locked tightly. The boy did not want to alarm his sister, but he was pretty much upset about the telephone call. After he had gone to bed he tossed from side to side, unable to sleep. Finally he got up and looked out of a window.

"A light!" he said, half aloud.

Off in the distance was a small moving light. Bert could not be sure whether it was on the road or in one of the fields.

"I'll get Nan," he thought, "and find out what she thinks."

He went across the hall to awaken his sister but she was not asleep. Like her brother, Nan was worrying that someone might try to enter the house.

"Come look out of my window," Bert urged her.

Together the twins hurried to the spot from which Bert had seen the light. There was not a sign of it now.

"Maybe the person who flashed the light is coming here," quavered Nan.

"Shall we go downstairs and watch?" suggested Bert.

"Let's wait a minute," Nan replied. "Maybe we'll see something else."

The next second the children saw an automobile moving along the side road. They thought surely it would stop near Mystery Mansion, but to their surprise the car went on. It had barely passed the lane into the house, when they saw a flickering light not far away. The beam seemed to be traveling through the gardens toward the pagoda.

"It's going away from the house, not coming here!" whispered Nan excitedly. "What do you make of that?"

Bert was stumped. As before, the light vanished. Then a few moments later a dim glow appeared high above the ground.

"What's that?" cried Nan.

"I'm sure I don't know," said Bert, "but it could have come from the roof of the pagoda."

His sister thought this was a very strange thing. How in the world could there be lights on the pagoda roof? Before she had a chance to figure out anything about it, the light vanished.

"Are you game to walk down there with me?" Bert asked her.

Nan did not want her brother to think she was afraid, so she said she would go along. Actually, the girl was fearful. It was pitch black outdoors, and the children were not very familiar with the grounds.

"I hope we don't fall into one of the pools," she whispered, as she left her brother's room to get dressed.

The twins hastily put on their clothes and met in the hall. Stealthily they tiptoed around the corner and down the back stairway.

"Why don't we just walk along the road?" suggested Nan. "It would be much easier than going through the gardens."

"All right," Bert agreed. "Oh!" he exclaimed suddenly. "I forgot to lock the door!"

Returning to the kitchen, he locked the door and

put the key in his pocket. The twins hastened across the lawn and then started down the road in the direction of the pagoda. There was not a sound anywhere. They began to wonder whether they were too late to find out who had been trespassing on Sing Foo's property.

About halfway to the Chinese pagoda Nan suddenly grabbed her brother's arm. "Did you see that?" she cried hoarsely.

"You mean the light?"

"Yes," the girl whispered.

Both children had seen a faint glow above the ground some distance ahead of them. They were sure it was near the roof of the pagoda. The rays vanished almost at once, and no light appeared in the garden or on the road.

"What do you make of it?" Nan asked her brother.

Bert replied it seemed as if some person must have gone around the other side of the pagoda with a flashlight, played it on the roof, then put it out.

"But why was he flashing it up there? And where is he now?" the boy wondered.

"Do you think he was the one who spoke to Flossie this evening?" Nan questioned her brother.

"I don't know," Bert said slowly, "but I believe the man who spoke to me on the telephone is the same one who spoke to Flossie."

The children hurried on in the darkness. They could not hear a sound. At the spot where the road ran about a hundred feet back of the pagoda, they walked up and down searching for a parked car, but could find none.

"Whoever was here must have gone away," Bert stated finally. "We'd better go back to the house now."

As they returned to the Mansion, the twins began to wonder if the whole episode was not the product of their imaginations. Yet someone had been walking through the gardens with a light; there was no doubt of that.

"Maybe we're silly to think he was planning any harm," Bert remarked as he and his sister entered the kitchen of Mystery Mansion.

"I'd think so too," said Nan, "if that mean old stranger hadn't threatened us. Do you think we ought to leave here, Bert?"

Her brother was quite sure they should not. He felt certain if Sing Foo had not wanted them to stay, he would not have invited them in the first place.

The twins returned to their beds, but found it impossible to fall asleep until dawn was in the sky. Then when they were sure no one would try to enter the house, they dozed off.

Although Bert and Nan slept late into the morning, Freddie and Flossie awoke at the usual time. The children dressed quietly and joined Aunt Sallie Pry in the kitchen where she was cooking breakfast. The elderly woman wanted to know where the older twins were. Flossie said:

"Nan hasn't wakened yet."

"This pan has bacon in it, yes," stated deaf Aunt

Sallie, misunderstanding what the twin had said.

Freddie and Flossie looked at each other. Then Freddie shouted loudly, "My brother's asleep still!"

"It's no bother," said Aunt Sallie. "Eat your fill."

The small twins gave up trying to make the woman understand. They helped her carry the breakfast into the dining room and the three of them sat down to eat. Aunt Sallie remarked that Bert and Nan must be very tired to stay in bed so late.

"We'll just wash up these dishes and start feeding the fish and birds without them," she announced.

Freddie and Flossie accompanied Mrs. Pry downstairs to the pools of tropical fish. After feeding them, the twins got seed and water for the birds which were in cages.

"Now be very careful," said Aunt Sallie. "We don't want any of them to get out."

Freddie and Flossie promised, though the woman could not hear them. She went off into another room, leaving the children to attend to the feeding.

"I guess this isn't bath day for the birds," said Flossie. "Maybe we—"

Freddie interrupted her with a shout, and made a dive for something. It was one of the birds!

"Oh! He's loose!" cried the little girl. "Why did you let him out?"

The escaped bird, which happened to be a very valuable canary, was flying around excitedly from place to place. Freddie did his best to capture the bird, but it was no use.

Flossie ran into the other room and summoned

Aunt Sallie. The woman gave one look and threw up her hands.

"Oh, Freddie, why did you do that?" she exclaimed. "We'll never be able to get the canary back!"

The small Bobbsey twin felt dreadful. He was trying his best to get the bird into its cage but was having no luck at all.

"Shut that door to the hall!" ordered Mrs. Pry.

Unfortunately Freddie did not reach it in time. The canary flew through the doorway and into the other part of the basement.

"Run up and close the door at the head of the stairs!" cried Aunt Sallie excitedly.

Again the bird got there first. By the time Freddie Bobbsey reached the top step, the canary had flown into the dining room and now was perched on a window frame.

The little boy hastened back to report this to Aunt Sallie. Grabbing the empty cage, the woman hurried up the stairway, but just as she reached the dining room the bird left the window frame and fluttered into the hall.

At this moment Bert Bobbsey, who was up now and had gone outdoors, was returning through the front door. As he opened it the canary flew out!

"Now you've done it!" cried Freddie.

Bert had seen a feathery object fly past him, but he had not guessed it was one of Sing Foo's prize possessions. Learning this, he turned around and hastened to the porch.

"Let me take the cage, Aunt Sallie," he said, as the bird perched itself among some vines.

Bert almost captured the canary but he was not quite quick enough. The little yellow bird excitedly flew from the vines and lit on the gutter of the porch roof.

"Now I'll get him!" cried the boy.

He leaped to the railing, climbed up the end post, and crawled along the roof toward the canary. The little bird was nearly exhausted. Never having been out of a cage before, it was frightened and confused. Bert was sure he could capture it now.

Half sitting on the roof, Bert edged himself along, his feet in the gutter. Suddenly there was a cracking sound. Before Bert Bobbsey knew what was happening, the gutter gave way.

The lad lost his balance and fell toward the ground!

CHAPTER XVIII

FLOSSIE FINDS A SHOW

HEARING the commotion outside, Nan Bobbsey looked from a second floor window. She was just in time to see her twin fall from the roof of the porch.

"Oh!" she exclaimed.

Hurrying down the stairs, the girl fully expected her brother to be badly hurt. She held her breath as she rushed from the house.

"Bert!" she cried.

The boy was just picking himself up from the ground with the help of Flossie, Freddie and Aunt Sallie. The three had been speechless with fright as Bert had hit the ground. Now they were relieved that he could get up.

"Are you—are you all right?" asked Nan, rushing to his side.

"Oh, sure," said Bert. But as he tried to take a few steps they all noticed that he limped considerably.

"You *are* hurt!" cried Aunt Sallie. "Is it—is it your leg?"

"I came down feet first," Bert explained. "I guess I twisted my ankle. But I'll walk around a little and

143

it'll be all right. Please don't worry about me."

"Why were you on the roof?" Nan asked him.

For a few moments the other children had forgotten about the escaped canary. Now they turned to see what had become of it. At first they could not locate the bird, but presently Flossie spied it perched on a tree branch.

"We'd better let the canary go," said Aunt Sallie. "I don't want any more accidents around here."

The children did not like this idea. They had heard that a bird brought up in captivity could not live out-of-doors like birds which were used to getting their own food and fighting for their own rights. They reminded Aunt Sallie of this.

"Please let me go up a ladder and try to capture the canary," Nan begged her.

Aunt Sallie merely shook her head. She said it was too bad the bird had got out, but she did not want to be responsible for anyone else getting hurt. Disheartened, the Bobbsey twins sat down to figure out how they might get hold of Sing Foo's pet without disobeying Mrs. Pry.

Freddie had an inspiration. He ran to the cellar of Mystery Mansion and got a shovel which he had seen there. Bringing it back to the garden he began to dig excitedly.

"Why are you doing that?" Flossie asked him.

"I'm hunting for worms," said the little boy.

Flossie understood at once. Birds like worms, and Freddie hoped to capture the canary by offering one to it.

"There's a worm!" the little girl cried suddenly.

Freddie picked up the wiggling object and slowly walked over to the tree where the little yellow bird was still perched. Looking up, the boy said quietly: "Here's some breakfast for you."

He held up the worm for the bird to see, then laid it on the ground. Backing away, he waited for the canary to descend. It took the bird so long to decide to do this that the worm had a chance to crawl several feet away and now was about to bury itself in the ground.

"Oh, please come down!" Freddie pleaded with the canary.

The small bird, apparently concluding that no harm would come to it, tremblingly fluttered toward the disappearing worm.

"Now!" whispered Freddie.

He grabbed up the empty cage which lay on the ground near by and tiptoed toward the unsuspecting bird. As it struggled to keep the worm from disappearing beneath the soil, the canary suddenly found a cage surrounding it. The Bobbseys sighed in relief.

Freddie was especially happy. Having been responsible for the bird's escape, he was glad to have been the one to capture it. He was sorry that Bert had hurt himself because of what he had done, and determined to be very good the rest of the day.

After the other birds had been fed, and Bert and Nan had finished a late breakfast, the Bobbsey twins decided to go on a hunt again for Sing Foo's Golden Key. So many things had happened it seemed like a long time since they had been on a search for it.

"Let's sep-rate," suggested Flossie. "Then we can cover more terr-tory."

The others agreed. The cellar where the furnace was and the basement containing the fish and birds were eliminated. It hardly seemed probable that Sing Foo would hide his precious key in such places.

"I'll take the front of the first floor this time," announced Bert, following Flossie's suggestion that they separate for the search. "Suppose you take the back, Nan."

"Freddie and I'll go upstairs," said Flossie. "He can take the front bedrooms and I'll take the back ones."

"Be very careful," Nan warned them as they started up the steps.

She herself went directly to the dining room. Although the children had eaten several meals here, none of them had ever looked through it thoroughly for any secrets. Nan began her search by peeking behind pictures, under rugs, inside drawers of the buffet, and in a Chinese cabinet which stood in a corner. It occurred to the Bobbsey girl that there could be false drawers in the furniture, so she spent several minutes searching for little springs and levers which might open them. Finding none, she sighed.

"I guess there are no secrets here after all," Nan told herself, "unless they're in that closet over there."

At one end of the room was a built-in closet with

a glass front. It contained several pieces of Oriental pottery. Carefully Nan picked these up, looking beneath and inside of them. No Golden Key was concealed anywhere.

While gazing at the back of the closet, the girl came to the realization that it was not an ordinary back. There was a knob on it. Perhaps this was a door with something hidden behind it!

Excitedly Nan removed the pieces of pottery from the closet. Then she leaned in and pulled on the knob. A door opened. Beyond was revealed a note which stood against a large black object. It said:

FOR THE ENJOYMENT OF THE BOBBSEY TWINS

"What can it be?" Nan thought, pulling the object toward her.

It proved to be a box, and when she lifted the lid, she discovered a moving picture projector inside. Nestled in a pocket beside it were two large rolls of film.

"I wonder what they are," Nan reflected, as she lifted the machine to the floor. "I must go tell the others."

Aunt Sallie was working in the kitchen, so Nan spoke to her first. Then she called Bert.

"I'll set it up right away," offered her twin when he saw the projector. "Call Freddie and Flossie, and we'll have a show."

The small twins clattered down the front stairway when they learned a moving picture show was

to be put on. One film was marked "Show this first."
The other said, "Show this last."

The Bobbsey boy set up the projector in the
strange room which held the chair that rocked by
itself and the statue that bobbed its head. This was
the darkest room in the house.

The moving picture projector was run by electric-
ity. Since Bert was familiar with handling a similar
one, he had no trouble in attaching the film. The
Bobbseys and Aunt Sallie watched eagerly as the
show began.

"Oh, it's in China!" cried Flossie excitedly. "Chinese children playing."

"Aren't they cute?" said Nan.

As the film progressed the twins laughed gaily.
The picture gave them a good idea of life in China,
and interspersed were many humorous scenes.

"Oh, I didn't know they have snow in China,"
said Freddie suddenly.

Nan laughed. She said there was plenty of snow
in China, but that this was not snow in the picture.
It was rice.

"But it's falling all over those children," cried
Freddie.

"They're throwing it at one another," said Nan.
"It must be some kind of game they're playing."

"I hope the children won't get spanked for wast-
ing the food," remarked Flossie, and this made the
others laugh.

The second film which Sing Foo had left proved
to be even more entertaining than the first one. It

was the story of the circus in which he had worked before coming to live in Lakeport.

"Sing Foo looked much younger then," remarked Aunt Sallie, as he was shown for a moment in a magician's costume. "Oh, my goodness!" she exclaimed suddenly.

A man now was swinging in the air from one trapeze to another! Flossie gave a little shriek and covered her eyes with her hands for a couple of seconds.

There followed some delightful scenes of bareback riders. In one act three clowns playfully annoyed the riders. The clowns attempted again and again to jump onto the horses, but each time they would miss and fall flat on the sawdust.

"They must be acrobats in disguise," remarked Nan. She told herself it did not hurt the men when they fell, although this was pretty hard to believe.

At the end of the act the bareback riders pretended to walk off in disgust. They left their horses running around the ring. The clowns, finding themselves alone, jumped to the animals' backs. After a little more nonsense they threw off their clown suits and lo! they were costumed as bareback riders! And Sing Foo was one of them!

"Gosh, he's marvelous!" said Bert.

Freddie and Flossie stood up and shouted in delight as one of the men jumped to the shoulders of another who was riding a horse around the ring. Then Sing Foo sprang to the second man's shoulders. Now the three of them were standing upright on the back of one horse, which still galloped madly around.

"Oh, I've never seen anything so wonderful!" cried Nan. "Now I know why Sing Foo knew how to rescue Flossie and Freddie when the horses ran away."

The interesting film ended with Sing Foo performing some of his tricks in a side show. A couple of them the Bobbsey twins already had seen, but there was one they hoped he would show them as soon as he should return from his trip. He was standing in a tiny snow-covered garden. Within a few seconds he made the snow melt, the plants peep out of the ground and in no time burst forth into bloom.

"I don't see how he does it," said Aunt Sallie.

"Show's over!" called Bert, noticing the film would soon come to an end.

"Oh, let's look at them both again!" cried Freddie.

Mrs. Pry thought it would be better to do this at another time, so Bert picked up the machine and put it back in the secret closet where Nan had found it. Since it was nearly lunch time the children voted to postpone their further search for the Golden Key until afternoon. But as soon as the smaller twins had finished their nap, they all started to hunt once more.

Flossie disappeared at once to the rear of the second floor. The little girl went straight to a certain room which she had been about to enter when called to the moving picture show. None of the twins had ever been inside this place, she was sure. Though it was dark, Flossie soon found a light and gazed around in awe.

"It's—it's a theater," she said aloud.

Truly it looked like one, only it was very small. There were no seats except a few chairs, but at the far end was a stage on which stood several figures.

Flossie almost expected to see them move, they looked so real. But she supposed they were only dolls. The little girl could not remember the names "marionettes" or "puppets," but she had been to several puppet shows. She recalled how someone behind the scenes pulls little strings attached to the figures to make them walk or dance.

"Oh, I wonder if these dollies work," the little girl said, half aloud. "I must find out."

Skipping to the stage, she pulled herself up and looked more closely at the puppets.

"Aren't they cute!" she thought.

At close range, Flossie could see the black strings attached to them. Carefully stepping around the figures, she found the board back of the stage where the strings were held in place on little hooks. It seemed to her as if there were hundreds of them.

"Oh, which is which?" she thought, deciding to see if the puppets would work.

Picking up the one nearest at hand, she suddenly lifted an old man right out of the garden in which he was standing. But a wheelbarrow he was pushing did not move, so Flossie tried another string. The wheelbarrow moved off by itself. Over and over again

Flossie pulled the various strings up and down, then sideways. But no matter how she worked them she could not make the old man walk along and push his wheelbarrow the way he was supposed to.

"I guess I'll try another one," the little girl sighed.

Near the edge of the stage stood a nurse holding a baby in her arms. Flossie finally figured out which strings belonged to them. The first one she pulled opened the baby's mouth. Flossie supposed this was how Sing Foo made the baby look as if it were crying. Pretending to be the magician, she spoke for the puppet, saying:

"Boo-hoo. Boo-hoo."

Next the little girl pulled a string tied to the baby's nurse, but the Bobbsey twin did something wrong and the nurse let the baby fall to the floor.

"Oh!" cried Flossie. "I hope I didn't break it."

She rushed from behind the scenes to find out. To her relief she discovered the baby was not harmed. It was made of wood like the other figures and could not break easily. Reassured, the little girl went back where the strings were tied and played there for a long time.

Presently Flossie discovered a large rope looped around a hook on the wall behind her. Wondering what this was for, she pulled on the rope. When nothing happened, the little girl decided to unwind it. Almost at once there was a grating sound and the child disappeared!

About this time the other children met in the

lower part of the house, as they had agreed to do. When Flossie did not appear, they became worried about her. Bert and Nan called her name loudly. Receiving no answer, they decided to go on a hunt for her.

It was some little time before they found the open door to the room where Flossie had located the little stage. As Bert peered into it he could see nothing but a few chairs. The marionette show which Flossie had found no longer was there!

The twins were about to leave the theater when they heard a muffled scream. Bert was sure it had come from his little sister Flossie!

CHAPTER XIX

THE MISSING TWINS

BERT, Nan and Freddie Bobbsey rushed into the room where the marionette show had been. Hurrying forward, they noticed a yawning cavity. Nan grabbed her small brother just in time to keep him from falling into it.

Again the children heard a muffled scream. They were positive it had come from Flossie.

"She must be down below," Bert surmised, trying to see what was beneath them.

It was impossible for the boy to make anything out of the mass of walls and other objects that made up the puppet stage.

"Flossie!" the boy cried. "Where are you?"

The little girl answered, but he could not make out her words. He asked her to repeat them. Still they seemed to make no sense. They sounded like "At the bottom in the theater with the dolls."

Bert told the words to Nan and Freddie but they could not understand what Flossie was talking about.

"Maybe she's in a back room," suggested Bert. "I'll see if I can get through. That looks like a door beyond the hole."

Holding tightly to a moulding on the side wall, the boy edged himself along the rim of the opening. He had almost reached the back of it when his hand accidentally pushed a button in the wall. Instantly a section of floor began to slide forward from the rear wall. It knocked Bert off balance and he fell into the black pit.

Nan cried out in horror. She tried to think of something she could do to help her brother, but before she could figure out anything the floor had covered the hole completely.

"Oh, Nan, what'll we do?" exclaimed Freddie. "Bert's gone and Flossie's gone!"

Nan felt like bursting into tears but she knew she must keep her head. Making Freddie promise to stay exactly where he was and not step on the new floor, she carefully tried it herself. Finding it would hold her weight, she crossed it quickly and opened the door Bert had spied at the rear of the room. Before going through, she called to Freddie:

"If Bert or Flossie or I don't come back in a few minutes, you go tell Mrs. Pry."

Too frightened to speak, the little boy merely nodded his head. Nan went on into the rear room, which was filled with puppets. For several moments the girl could not figure out why they were there. Then a thought came to her.

"Flossie must have been on a disappearing stage," she decided, "and Bert fell down onto it, too. I must get them out!"

But how was Nan to do this? First of all, she

would have to find the secret combination to make the floor roll back. She decided it must be near the place where Bert had been standing when he lost his balance. But try as she might, the girl could not locate it.

In her excitement Nan had forgotten all about Freddie. The little boy had not waited for her to come back. He had hurried down the stairs and told Aunt Sallie what had happened. Freddie had screamed his dreadful news so loudly that she had had no trouble understanding him.

"Oh, my goodness!" the woman cried. "Mystery Mansion is getting to be too much for me. Show me where the children are."

"I can't," Freddie yelled at her. "They're all gone!"

When he led Aunt Sallie into the little theater they saw Nan there, and learned that she was trying to find something by which she could open up the floor again. But the girl could not locate the secret push button.

Getting down on their knees, the three of them pushed with all their might against the movable floor, but it would not budge an inch. Shouting through the crack, Nan called her brother's name, but he did not answer.

"Maybe——maybe Bert hurt himself," quavered Freddie, "and can't answer you."

Nan was afraid this might be true. She was at her wits' end to know what to do, and appealed to Aunt Sallie to figure out something.

In the meantime Bert had picked himself up and was feeling around in the pitch blackness. On every side of him were objects of various kinds. He could not identify them, because they were pieces of scenery. To his touch they did not mean trees or walls.

As Bert came near one of the marionettes, he almost cried aloud. It seemed so human! The boy might have become unnerved in the mysterious atmosphere if he had not suddenly heard Flossie wail.

"Where are you?" Bert cried.

"Here!" the small twin answered. "I'm stuck behind something and I can't get out. Where are you?"

Of course, Bert could not tell her, but guided by her voice, and pushing aside various objects in his path, he finally reached his small sister's side.

"Oh, Bert!" the little girl sobbed in relief, clinging to her brother. "I want to get out!"

"So do I!" he said, "but I haven't the least idea how. I don't even know what kind of a place I'm in. Do you?"

"I think so," she replied.

Flossie explained about the little stage which had gone down with her. This only made matters worse. The boy suddenly realized that probably the stage was open on all four sides. It was only by good fortune that neither he nor Flossie had fallen off into space!

Bert suggested that the little girl sit very still while he walked around to investigate. Feeling his way inch by inch, he went around the four edges of the stage, discovering that while three were open, the back had a partition. It was because of this that Flossie had not fallen off.

"Where are you?" the little girl cried out suddenly.

"I'm right here," said Bert. "Don't be frightened."

"But when are you going to get us out?" she demanded.

"I'm doing my best," the boy replied. Looking upward, he shouted as loudly as possible:

"Nan! Nan!"

From above there came a muffled reply. He was sure it was his twin's voice. The boy yelled, hoping she could hear him:

"Push—the—button—on—the—wall!"

Bert waited for the ceiling above him to roll back. When nothing happened, he repeated his words, telling the exact location of the button. Again he waited. Then finally a crack of light appeared and slowly the ceiling began to move. A moment later Nan shouted down:

"Are you all right?"

Bert called that he and Flossie were not hurt. He did not know how they were going to get up into the room, however, since there was nothing on which to climb.

Flossie came forward and tried to explain what had made the stage descend. She told of unwinding a rope at the back of the stage. Bert scooted behind the scenery, but here it was dark and he could not see the rope.

"Get Sing Foo's flashlight on the hall table, will you, Nan?" he called up.

His twin sped off, and soon returned with the light. She tossed it down to her brother, and a couple of minutes later the boy shouted that he could see the rope but he could not figure out how to reach the end of it.

"It's dangling somewhere up above," he announced.

"Maybe there's something in the back room," cried Nan. "I wonder if I can get to it."

A few minutes before, when the floor had begun to move out of sight, she had sped across it to safety. Now the only way to get to the back room would be by going along the rim of the hole, as Bert had tried to do. Could she make it without falling below?

"I'll have to try," she determined. "I can't leave Bert and Flossie down there."

Inch by inch the Bobbsey girl pulled herself along the side of the opening. She made the rear wall in safety and went through to the back room. On a wall she found a small wheel with a crank on it.

"This must be it!" she thought, and slowly turned the crank.

There was a grating sound, and a moment later the stage began to rise. Everyone held his breath, hoping nothing would go wrong before Bert and Flossie could be hauled to safety.

Lifting the stage was dreadfully hard work for Nan. Several times she felt as if she could not move the crank another inch. Out of breath, and straining every muscle, the girl paused several times, fearful that the weight would jerk the wheel from her hand.

At last, however, the stage was in place. Quickly Bert tied the heavy rope to the hook on the back wall. Nan was so exhausted she could no longer stand up. When her twin dashed into the back room to thank his sister for the rescue, he gazed at her in alarm. She was deathly white and could not speak.

"Nan, what happened to you?" her brother cried.

Poor Nan could not answer him. But she smiled weakly. Bert began to rub her wrists vigorously, and finally she sat up, declaring she was all right. She assured him that if she just had a drink of water she would feel fine.

Bert ran off to get this, and in a little while he and Nan, as well as the others, went down to the first floor of Mystery Mansion. For a while they sat on the front porch resting and talking over their adventure. Freddie had just remarked that none of them had found the Golden Key yet, when they saw an automobile turn into the driveway.

"It's our car!" cried Bert. "Oh!" he said suddenly, "I guess we have to go home."

The twins fully expected that their mother and father were arriving and would tell them to pack up their clothes. It was a surprise, therefore, to find Sam was at the wheel, with Dinah beside him.

At once the four children went down the porch steps to greet the kind Negroes. Nan inquired if her parents were all right.

"Yes, dey's fine. Gone out fo' de evenin', though,"

announced Dinah, "so I come out heah to git yo' supper."

"That'll be fun," said Nan. "Then Aunt Sallie can rest."

"May we stay until nine o'clock?" Flossie asked.

Sam and Dinah grinned. "Shall we tell de chilluns now?" questioned Sam. "I nevah did see no sense to keepin' good news." Then with a twinkle in his eyes he announced, "Yo' school am goin' to be closed tomorrow."

"Whoops!" cried Freddie, and turned a somersault.

"You mean we don't have to go to school?" questioned Flossie, her eyes opening very wide.

"Dat's right," said Dinah.

Sam grinned broadly, showing all his beautiful white teeth.

"Why don't yo' tell dem de best news ob all?" he asked his wife Dinah.

" 'Cause I'd like to keep it fo' a little surprise," the cook replied. "But ef yo' wants to tell dem, go ahead."

The twins begged to know what the rest of the secret was. They danced around in delight when they heard that Mr. and Mrs. Bobbsey had given permission for them to stay at Mystery Mansion one more day if they wished to.

"If we wish to!" yelled Bert. "Wowee! Another whole day to hunt for the Golden Key!"

The small twins led Sam and Dinah into the house, trying to tell them all the things which had happened. The old Negroes had to admit that life at Mystery Mansion certainly had been exciting.

"I believes yo' all ought to settle down now and jest be quiet while I cooks yo' a good meal," said Dinah.

The children never tired of watching their faithful cook prepare a meal, so they all trooped to the kitchen with her to watch and help. Suddenly Nan realized that Aunt Sallie was not present. Then she knew why. The poor woman was feeding the fish and the birds all alone!

Dinah insisted that she did not need the twins to help her so they went off to the basement. Mrs. Pry was almost through with her work, so it was not long before the Bobbseys returned to the kitchen.

Sam was sitting in a corner looking at some money which he held in his hand. The elderly man was shaking his head.

"Is something the matter?" Nan asked him.

To her amazement as well as Bert's he replied, "Dis yere bill is no good."

"You mean it's a counterfeit!" Bert cried excitedly.

"Dat's what dey tells me."

The children demanded to know where Sam had got the fake money. He explained that the five-dollar bill had been given to him the day before. He had not known that it was no good until he had tried to buy something with it at a store.

"It's a shame," said Nan. "Does Daddy know about this?"

"Yes, I told him," Sam announced. "An' he done repo'ted to de police where I got it."

At this instant Dinah broke into the conversation. She remarked that it was a shame nowadays "how a pusson can't do nothin'."

"What do you mean?" Bert and Nan asked together.

The elderly cook told how she and Sam had been stopped on the road just before entering the grounds of Mystery Mansion. A man had insisted that they not drive in.

"But I done told him I was comin' in anyway," spoke up Sam angrily. "Nobody was goin' to keep me away from de Bobbsey twins."

"He was trying to keep you away from us?" asked Bert excitedly.

Sam explained the stranger had insisted no one was living at Mystery Mansion. He had said he owned the place and was not going to let anyone visit it.

Bert and Nan exchanged glances. Could the stranger have been the same man who had telephoned the evening before, ordering them out of the house? If so, the dreadful man was still around!

CHAPTER XX

STRANGE LIGHTS

THE older Bobbsey twins wondered whether they should tell Sam and Dinah about the mysterious telephone call the night before. While they were thinking this over, Dinah told them that supper was ready and asked them to come to the table right away.

"Hot soup should be eaten hot," the kind cook stated firmly. "Cold soup's no good."

Laughing, the twins hurried to the dining room with Aunt Sallie. Dinah served one of the most delicious meals she had ever prepared; cream of tomato soup, toasted club sandwiches with crisp bacon, and hot prune pudding with vanilla sauce.

By way of thanks to the cook, Bert asked Dinah if she would like to watch a little show. When the woman said nothing would please her better, the boy announced the performance would be ready in twenty minutes.

"You and Sam and everybody else go to the room where Sing Foo put on his show," Bert said, and then disappeared upstairs.

The boy was very mysterious about what he was doing. He would let none of the other twins watch him. Over a week before, Sing Foo had told the boy where the magician's costume was kept. Now Bert found the outfit and struggled to pull it on over his other clothes.

"This is the queerest suit I've ever seen," he thought.

There were so many pockets in the trousers that at first the lad could not see the openings through which he was supposed to step. And the long coat which went over them had such bulky linings in the sleeves it was difficult for Bert to get his arms through them. Finally when he was dressed, the boy set the magician's special cap on his head. Here again he had to proceed carefully, because the cap was full of wires and secret pockets. Bert wished Sing Foo had left the toy mouse which crawled up and down the queue, but the man had put away all the gadgets he employed in his tricks.

"Sing Foo meant me to use the things in this box, though," Bert told himself, picking up a fan and a little flower pot. There was a note on each one.

When Bert Bobbsey, Magician, thought he was ready, he looked at himself in a mirror. Something was wrong. What was it?

"Oh, I know," the boy laughed. "I forgot the long mustache."

Opening the closet door once more he took this out and stuck it on above his lips. Then, glancing at himself in the mirror again, he was sure he looked enough like Sing Foo to put on a show.

Bert's audience was already seated when the boy

walked into the room. "Ching-a-ling, ching-a-ling," he called out. His disguise was so good that at first only Nan recognized him as one of the twins.

Now Bert did not know a single Chinese word, but he rubbed his hands together and made several strange sounds just as if he knew the language. Then he said, trying to imitate Sing Foo's voice:

"Watch carefully!"

The boy whirled around, and from his sleeve there appeared a small fan. The young magician opened it. The fan looked like any other. He asked Nan to come forward to examine it.

"Do you see anything strange about this?" he asked her, acting just as the real magician had.

Nan pronounced the fan to be a regular one. Bert began to pull it out sideways like an accordion. It grew bigger and bigger.

"Oh!" cried Flossie. "You'll break the fan!"

But the fan did not break, even though Bert stretched it out until it was six feet long.

"Oh, it's a giant's fan!" exclaimed Freddie. "Can you make it small again?"

Bert pretended that it would be very hard to do this, but slowly he brought his hands together. In a minute the fan was normal in size.

"Oh, please let me try it!" cried Freddie, jumping from his chair.

The boy magician handed the fan to him, but try as he might, Freddie could not make it any bigger. Bert had learned his lesson well from the instructions Sing Foo had put on the note!

As the Bobbsey boy concluded his trick, Sam and Dinah clapped loudly. They wondered who the magician was. It was not very light in the room, and they had not caught on yet to his identity.

Suddenly from Bert's sleeve a tiny flower pot appeared. He asked Nan if she would run to the kitchen and bring him a small glass of water. While the girl was gone, he walked over to Dinah and requested that she hold the flower pot.

"Is this not a regular flower pot, Madam?" he asked, disguising his voice.

Now there was one thing which Bert could not disguise. That was his eyes! Dinah looked up at him. There was no mistaking those twinkling brown eyes, but Dinah did not let on she had guessed who the boy magician was.

"Dis yere flower pot looks puffectly no'mal to me, suh," she replied.

By this time Nan had returned. She handed the glass of water to Bert, who in turn offered it to Dinah.

"Please, Madam, sprinkle a little water on the earth in this flower pot," he asked her.

Dinah did as requested.

"The power of water is wonderful," the boy magician went on.

Freddie and Flossie had slid out of their seats, and now crowded around to see what would happen. Suddenly, before the eyes of them all a little leaf appeared on the surface of the earth in the flower pot.

"Will Madam please put on a little more water?" Bert requested.

Dinah sprinkled some drops on the growing plant. Within a few seconds it pushed itself still farther above the earth. As they all looked on, fascinated, it became a plant. In ten more seconds pink flowers blossomed at the ends of the stems.

Just as Freddie was about to pick off one of the flowers, Bert whisked the pot from Dinah's hand, turned around, and walked to the side of the room. When he turned back once more to face his audience the flower pot had disappeared!

"Oh, where did it go?" cried Flossie.

The boy magician merely smiled. He did not intend to give away Sing Foo's secrets, so he pretended not to hear what the little girl had said.

Nan guessed that the flower pot trick had been made possible by using paper flowers which expanded in water. Then, too, while holding the fan, she had felt a small catch which held the leaves in place, so she had solved that mystery, too.

Bert now was gazing intently across the room. As the others looked in the same direction, they became startled. Surely Bert had nothing to do with what was happening!

The chair which rocked all by itself was now rocking vigorously!

Dinah gave a little scream, and Sam said "Lawsy me!"

The small twins, who had felt that Sing Foo in some way had been responsible for the rocking of

the chair, were completely puzzled now and not a
little frightened at the way it was acting. Nan rushed
to her twin's side and whispered:

"Bert, do you think something's the matter?"

Her brother did not reply. He walked over to the
mysterious chair, but by the time he got there it had
stopped rocking.

Lightly the boy magician touched it, but the chair
remained motionless. No one could understand what
had happened to cause it to rock.

While they were discussing the incident the young
magician disappeared upstairs. Quickly he pulled off
Sing Foo's costume from over his other clothes, put
it away, and hurried down again. As he reached the
bottom of the steps, Flossie gave a shriek. Then she
laughed softly.

"Now I know!" she exclaimed.

Bert wondered why his small sister was making
such a fuss. He tried to act very dignified, and asked
her what was the matter.

"Your mustache!" she cried out. "It's still on!"

Bert realized that in his hurry he had forgotten
to remove it. He was a funny sight indeed! Catching
a glimpse of himself in the mirror, the boy too
laughed merrily, then went back upstairs to put away
Sing Foo's mustache.

Meanwhile Dinah had told Flossie and Freddie
to go to bed. She said she would wash the dishes and
clean up the kitchen, then she and Sam would leave.

Nan asked Sam if he would walk outside with her
and Bert. The girl told him about the strange light

they had seen the night before, and wondered if it might appear again.

"You forget it was much later than this when we saw it," Bert reminded his sister.

"But things might have been going on before that time," Nan insisted. "Maybe we just didn't notice them earlier."

"Dinah an' I am in no special hurry," said Sam. "We kin wait a while. Mebbe we should anyway if dere's somethin' dangerous goin' on around heah."

"We don't know whether it's dangerous or not," said Bert, "but it's surely mysterious."

"We thought maybe a burglar was stealing some of Sing Foo's things—or at least trying to," explained Nan.

About ten o'clock Sam, Bert and Nan walked slowly through the gardens toward the pagoda. For a while there was not a light nor a sound anywhere; then suddenly Nan whispered:

"Look! On the road!"

Coming toward them in the opposite direction from Lakeport was a car.

"Do you suppose it's going to stop?" the girl asked excitedly.

Sam advised that they stand still and watch. As the automobile reached a point in line with the pagoda it suddenly veered off sharply, and came to a halt. Its lights then went out.

"There's no road over there," announced Bert. "That car must have been driven into a field. Let's find out."

Sam and Nan held him back as he started off. They felt more could be learned by waiting.

"If some men are coming to the pagoda or the house we'll hear them," the girl said.

They all fully expected to see the beam of a flashlight, but none appeared. Tiptoeing cautiously toward the Chinese building, the three were startled to hear a sound very much like the squeaking of a door.

"Maybe someone went into the pagoda," whispered Bert tensely. "Let's find out!"

Together the three stole forward. Bert tried the door. It was locked!

"I guess no one came in here after all," he said. "Let's walk over toward the car."

In order to do this they had to cover the distance from the pagoda to the road as well as several feet into the field beyond. As they neared the parked automobile Sam insisted the twins remain where they were. He would investigate alone.

"I don't want yo' all to get in trouble," he said.

Upon reaching the car the old Negro found it empty and summoned the twins. Bert and Nan could faintly make out the license number and memorized it. Then slowly they started away, wondering where the passengers had gone, and why.

"Maybe they went up the road to Mystery Mansion!" said Nan fearfully. "We'd better go back there and find out."

"We sure had," Bert agreed.

The three hurried along the road. Just before

reaching the house Bert turned around. He stopped and asked the others to look.

"Do you see what I see?" he cried in a hoarse whisper. "Near the roof of the pagoda."

For a few seconds they could make out the same reflection the twins had noticed the night before. Then it vanished.

"What do you make of that, Sam?" Nan asked.

Sam was trembling with excitement and apprehension. He did not want the Bobbsey children to know how he felt, but this place was entirely too spooky for him, he had decided. The man announced he thought all of them should leave Mystery Mansion and go back to their safe home right away.

"But it's perfectly safe here," said Bert. "Nothing has happened to us."

"Yo' never kin tell when somethin' might," said the old Negro.

"It would be dreadful to run away from Sing Foo's mansion when he expects us to help Aunt Sallie," stated Bert manfully.

Sam admitted that there was something to this. He finally promised to say nothing to Dinah about the twins going home.

"The car! It's leaving!" cried Nan suddenly.

This was true. Whoever had left the automobile parked in the field now had put on the headlights, turned the car around, and was speeding up the road toward them.

"Maybe we can stop them!" cried Bert. "I'll bet they stole something from the pagoda!"

Before the others could restrain the boy he had stepped into the road and begun to shout and wave his arms wildly.

The driver of the automobile, instead of stopping, put on a burst of speed and raced past Sam and the Bobbsey twins.

CHAPTER XXI

DANNY'S FRIGHT

BERT, Nan and Sam stared after the disappearing automobile. There seemed to be two men in it.

"I'm sure they're thieves!" cried Bert.

Sam did not agree, saying the men had not had time to do any stealing. But Nan argued that they might have had a package in the pagoda all ready to take out when they came there.

"I don' like dis place," said Sam, as the three walked toward Mystery Mansion. "I really believes yo' all bettah come home with me."

It took several minutes to convince the elderly Negro it would not be kind of the twins to leave Aunt Sallie Pry so abruptly. They pointed out the fact they ought to help her guard Sing Foo's property.

"Please let us stay one more day," Nan pleaded. "I'm sure we'll be all right. And we haven't found the Golden Key yet, either."

"What's dat?" Sam asked.

When Nan explained how Sing Foo had told them a Golden Key which would unlock some of his treasures was hidden in Mystery Mansion, the old man grinned and remarked he could not blame the twins for wanting to find it.

"I went diggin' fo' a treasure once when I was a little boy," he said.

"Did you find anything?" Bert wanted to know.

Sam shook his head. "De boy what told me about de treasure was only foolin'. I dug an' dug till mah back ached, but all I evah found was a lot o' stones."

As soon as they reached the house Dinah said she and Sam must leave. The couple climbed into the automobile, waved good-by to the twins, and warned them to be careful. Sam then started off.

"We'll come an' fetch yo' tomorrow," called Dinah.

"I hopes yo' finds de key," Sam said, leaning out of the car window.

Though the search for the mysterious key was uppermost in the children's minds as they went to bed, in the morning it was completely forgotten because of something else which happened. Aunt Sallie and the twins had just finished eating breakfast when they heard a commotion outside the Mansion.

"It's Smoky!" cried Flossie. "Something's happened to her!"

The little girl had put the kitten outdoors. Now it was meowing loudly.

"It's her fright cry!" exclaimed Flossie, and ran from the table.

What a sight met her eyes as she rushed to the front porch! In the garden stood a boy. He was holding poor Smoky by her tail and swinging her round and round in a circle as fast as he could.

"Danny Rugg! You stop that!" screamed Flossie as she raced down the steps.

Bert, Nan and Freddie had followed their small sister. When Bert saw what was happening he did not wait to run down the stairs. He jumped the full length of them.

"Put her down!" he yelled at the bully.

Seeing the glint in Bert's eyes, Danny gave Smoky a fling. As the kitten landed in a flower-bed, Flossie rushed to her side.

"I didn't hurt her," Danny said, when Bert came forward as if to fight him.

"I'm not so sure you didn't," said Bert, glaring at the bully. "Nan can find that out. I'll settle with you!"

"Want to fight, eh?" said the bully. "Well, I'm not going to fight you. I'd only lick you anyway."

It is probable there would have been a fight then and there if Aunt Sallie had not come from the house at this very moment. She had not heard Flossie's exclamation at the breakfast table, but she sensed something was wrong and had come to find out about it. Seeing Bert double up his fists and move toward Danny Rugg, she called out to him:

"Stop!"

Freddie told the woman what the bully had done. While Aunt Sallie agreed Danny deserved a licking she said she wanted no fights around Mystery Mansion.

This was just what Danny wanted to hear! Now

that he knew he was not to get a black eye or a bloody nose, he began to sneer.

"You're still a little kid, aren't you, Bert?" he taunted, a leering grin on his face. "Have to have a nurse take care of you, eh?"

Bert Bobbsey was furious. It was all he could do to keep from striking the other boy, but he did not want to displease Aunt Sallie. Holding his temper, he said:

"You mind your own business, Danny Rugg. What are you doing out here anyway? You weren't invited."

"Oh," Danny replied loudly to be sure everyone would hear him, "I just came to find out how the passer of bad money is."

This was too much for Bert. Since he had not been guilty of deliberately trying to use the counterfeit five-dollar bill, he could not stand this insult. Like lightning his arm shot out and caught Danny square on the chest. The bully staggered back.

"S-stop that!" shouted Aunt Sallie, running down the steps toward the two boys. "I said I would have no fighting and I mean it!"

"Oh, Bert, please mind Aunt Sallie!" cried Nan, rushing toward her twin. "Smoky isn't hurt and nobody but Danny believes you'd try to pass bad money."

"What do you mean, he wouldn't try to?" said Danny. "He sure would, and so would your father."

At this remark Nan too became furious, but much as the Bobbsey twins would have liked teaching

Danny Rugg a lesson, they were not permitted to do so. Aunt Sallie was very firm. She asked the visitor why he had come.

"To get you all out of here," he said.

"I never bet and I have no auto here," Aunt Sallie replied. "What are you talking about?"

Danny looked puzzled. Nan finally told him the woman was deaf, and suggested he shout loudly to make her understand.

Danny took the hint. "I came to tell you," he repeated, "YOU HAVE TO GET OUT!"

"I can hear you," said Aunt Sallie. "But what is it you want me to get out?"

The Bobbseys never minded Aunt Sallie's mistakes, but Danny was annoyed. He remarked he didn't see how the twins could stand having Mrs. Pry around. Bert came to the kind woman's defense.

"If anybody is going to get out of here it's going to be you, Danny Rugg!" he said.

"Is that so? Well, maybe if I tell you something, you'll change your mind."

"What do you mean?" Bert asked him.

"I mean that if you don't leave this house—every one of you—you're going to be arrested!" Danny threw back his head and laughed. "You twins certainly would look funny behind the bars of a jail."

Bert and Nan were so surprised at what the bully had said they did not reply for several seconds. Freddie and Flossie came close to their older brother and sister.

"What does he mean, Nan?" asked Flossie tremulously. "We haven't done anything wrong here."

"Of course we haven't," Nan comforted her. "Danny's just trying to scare us."

"No, I'm not," said the boy. "I know it's true."

"Then you'd better tell us what you're talking about," said Bert, his eyes flashing. "And make it quick!"

Danny was willing. He related how he had met a man in Lakeport the evening before. The stranger had asked him if he knew the Bobbsey twins. When Danny had answered that he did, the man had inquired if the boy would do an errand for him.

"He told me you were out here," Danny went on. "He said I should come and tell you he owns this house now. He's already asked you to get out but you didn't do it. Now he's going to have you arrested if you don't go."

Bert and Nan looked at each other. This was serious! They had no doubt but that Danny was telling the truth, but wondered why he had consented to coming. They soon found out. The strange man had paid the bully well to do the errand! Danny had ridden out on a highway bus and then walked the rest of the way to the Mansion.

"Before you move out," said Danny, "I want you to show me the house."

"We're not going to move," stated Bert flatly.

"You were a mean boy to swing my Smoky around," spoke up Flossie. "You don't deserve to see the house."

Suddenly Bert had an idea. He had not been able

to teach Danny a lesson by fighting him. Maybe he could punish the boy by scaring him with some of the tricks in the house! Winking at Nan, he said:

"All right, Danny, I'll show you the house. But we'll have to make it snappy."

The bully followed the Bobbsey boy inside. He was sure now Bert was afraid of him, and for this reason had not dared to refuse his request. Bert, a little fearful the small twins might give away the secrets of Mystery Mansion, suggested that they help Aunt Sallie. She already had gone to feed the birds and fish. They eagerly ran off to the basement.

The first room which Bert showed Danny was the one containing the mysterious rocking chair and the statue which bobbed its head. After pointing out some of the interesting objects which stood about, Bert suggested that Danny put his hand on the statue.

"See how smooth and beautiful the face is," he egged the bully on.

Danny was not gentle in the way he touched the head, and it began to bob instantly. Danny stepped back in surprise. A moment later the man's arm began to rise, almost touching the boy. Then the statue started speaking.

Danny was upset. Quickly he backed away to the door.

"What's the matter?" asked Nan, trying hard to keep from laughing.

"Th-that statue," Danny stammered. "It must be a-a-alive!"

Bert and Nan pretended they could not understand this. They walked over to the statue, gazed at it, and told Danny he must be seeing things. The statue certainly was not alive!

"It isn't even moving," stated Nan.

Danny, who never had heard about Mystery Mansion, could not figure out what had happened. He began to wonder himself whether he was seeing things. Bert whispered to Nan to go upstairs and put the lights on in the theater.

Now he called Danny's attention to the attractive furniture in the room. The visitor's eyes roved about. Then suddenly he cried out.

Across the room a chair was rocking all by itself!

"What's the matter?" Bert asked the bully. "Did you see something?"

"Th—that chair," said Danny, pointing. "It's rocking!"

"Why, how could it?" asked Bert. "No one's in it!"

"It—it rocked itself," said Danny.

Now the chair was standing perfectly still, and Bert brought this fact to Danny's attention. The bully just stared. He was sure the chair had rocked. But why didn't Bert seem to know this, he wondered.

"Come on, I'll show you the rest of the house," Bert invited him. "Suppose we go upstairs."

The Bobbsey boy went straight to the room which held the disappearing stage. He explained to Danny that the man who owned the house sometimes put on little plays with puppets. As Danny stalked across the room, Bert whispered something to Nan. She nodded, and stayed near the door. Bert crossed the room and pointed out the various objects on the stage.

"Go up and look them over," he suggested to Danny.

Unaware that anything would happen to him, the mean boy stepped onto the stage and began picking up the different objects. Bert disappeared into the room back of the stage.

Suddenly the lights went out. At the same moment Danny felt the floor under him give way.

"Help! Help!" he cried.

There was not a sound. He called first for Bert, then for Nan, but they did not answer him. The floor kept on going down and down.

What was happening? Where was he going?

"Help! Help!" cried Danny again.

When Bert thought the bully had had enough of a scare to punish him for his meanness, he turned the crank on the wall and wound up the rope which controlled the stage. As soon as the floor was in place once more, he scooted out where the puppets stood and gave a low whistle. Nan turned on the lights.

"What were you making so much noise about, Danny?" Bert asked the bully. "Did one of the puppets grab you?"

Danny was still shaking with fright. It did not dawn on him that Bert had played a trick on him.

"You know why I cried out," he said solemnly.

"You felt this floor go down and the lights go out as well as I did."

"The floor went down and the lights went out?" Bert asked. "Why, what made you think that?"

Danny did not know what to think. Of one thing he was quite sure: either he was crazy, or this was a very strange house. In any case, he decided to leave at once, and asked Bert to show him the front door. The Bobbsey boy was only too delighted to do this!

After Danny had gone, Bert and Nan laughed so hard they had to sit down for a while. They concluded that getting square with the mean boy in this fashion was a lot better than fighting him.

"I'll bet he won't come back, either," said Bert. From a window he had noticed Danny Rugg running up the road as fast as his legs could carry him!

CHAPTER XXII

NAN'S DISCOVERY

"WE'D better go help Aunt Sallie now," suggested Nan, getting up from her chair.

She and Bert started for the basement. The fish already had been fed. Now Aunt Sallie and the small twins were busy giving the birds their breakfast.

"I want to feed the big birds," stated Flossie, and picked up the bag of seed for them.

Upon reaching the cage in the next room, where the big unfriendly birds were walking around, the little girl threw in a handful of the seed. Then she set down the bag and pressed her face between two of the bars to watch. Becoming more and more interested, she gradually pushed her whole head through, forgetting entirely that the birds were not friendly, and that anyone going into the cage had to wear a mask.

Two long-legged flamingos suddenly began to fight over the food. Flossie scolded them. Looking up, they saw her little face inside the cage. Instantly they flapped their wings and came straight at her. When she started to pull her head back, she found it would not budge!

The angry birds tried to peck the little girl's face. Flossie beat them off as best she could, but they scratched her face and hands.

"Go 'way!" she screamed.

The other birds in the cage set up a terrific din. The noise of their cries, combined with those of the child, brought the other twins running to her side. Each one tried to help her, but it seemed impossible to get Flossie's head from between the bars. Realizing this, Bert dashed to the closet where the costume he wore in the cage was kept. He grabbed up the helmet and quickly put it over Flossie's head.

Nan meanwhile had seized a broom and was waving it in front of the angry birds to keep them from making any further attacks on her little sister. She instructed Freddie to run for Mrs. Pry.

"Oh, my gracious!" exclaimed the deaf woman when the little boy brought her into the room.

For a second she could not think what to do. Then she recalled something she had once seen her mother do, when a cat had wedged its head into a pitcher of milk, and been unable to get it out. Quickly Mrs. Pry got a cake of soap from a near-by sink and greased the cage bars on either side of Flossie's head to make them slippery. Next she filled a pan with cold water. Instructing Bert to pull off Flossie's helmet, she dashed the water onto the little girl's hair. The poor twin, frightened, gave a quick jerk and pulled her head through the bars!

"Oh, thank goodness!" said Aunt Sallie. "I didn't know whether it would work or not."

Flossie, who had burst into tears, was clinging tightly to Nan.

"Oh! Oh!" she sobbed. "I never want to see those awful birds again!"

"Come with me," her sister said kindly. "I'll fix up the scratches on your face and hands."

She led Flossie away. Aunt Sallie offered to go along, but Nan assured her she could attend to it alone.

"All right," said Mrs. Pry. "I guess I'd better see what I can do with these birds."

All of them were fighting among themselves, and the squawking was terrific. Aunt Sallie tried hard to remember what Sing Foo had told her to do in such an emergency.

It was Freddie who saved the day. He had often heard his mother and Dinah remark that lots of times when children are out of sorts, it's because they're hungry. The little boy was sure this was what was the matter with the herons, the flamingos and the other big birds. As fast as he could, he threw handfuls of the seed between the bars of the cage. Wisely he did not throw it all in one spot but scattered it over the entire floor. One by one the big birds began to eat, and in a few minutes all the fighting ceased.

"Good for you, Freddie," Bert praised his little brother.

He offered to put on the protective suit and go into the cage with fresh water, but Aunt Sallie thought it would be best not to attempt this yet.

Some water still remained in the pans, and she said this would have to do until the birds quieted down. Now that the fighting was over, Mrs. Pry recalled one thing Sing Foo had told her to do in case of a fight—turn out all the lights!

She told the boys about it, and they put the big room in darkness. Then they closed the door and went upstairs.

"I believe I'll telegraph Sing Foo to come home," said Aunt Sallie wearily. "This place really is too much for me."

"If you telegraph—" Bert said.

"Take a bath?" Aunt Sallie asked, looking surprised.

Bert smiled and repeated, "If you do telegraph Sing Foo, ask him if he has sold this house."

"Ask him how old his mouse is?"

The Bobbsey boy patiently repeated his request. The deaf woman laughed at her mistake, and said she would be glad to find out if the Chinese had sold Mystery Mansion and whether they all should leave at once.

In the meantime Nan had gently bathed Flossie's scratches and put some soothing salve on them. The little girl, still shaken from her adventure, decided to go outdoors and lie in one of the hammocks. Nan found an interesting picture book for her, but after turning a few of the pages the little girl fell asleep.

As Bert and Freddie seemed to be busy, Nan decided to go on a search by herself for some of Sing Foo's secrets. There were many spots still to be explored. Going back to the second floor of Mystery Mansion, the girl peered into the various bedrooms.

"No, I'll not look here again," she thought. "We examined them all pretty carefully."

She walked on and turned the corner into the hallway leading to the back stairs. All the doors along it were closed, and Nan could not recall which of the rooms already had been explored by the twins.

"I don't even remember this door," she told herself, noticing one with Chinese writing on it. "I wonder if it's locked."

The door opened easily, however, and the girl went in.

"Oh!" she gasped. "How wonderful!"

The place was a treasure trove! On one wall hung hundreds of beautifully carved swords of various shapes and sizes. Several had ivory handles, while others were studded with jewels.

On a small table were several delicately carved jade animals. Beautiful silken scarves were draped gracefully over chair backs.

In cabinets and on tables lay musical instruments of various kinds. Nan had never seen any quite like them, and she assumed they were used only in China. One, however, she did know about from her studies in school. It was a three-stringed Chinese fiddle. Picking it up, the girl strummed a few notes. They echoed weirdly through the strange room.

A group of games on a stand now caught Nan's eye. She did not know the names of any of them except Mah Jong, and wondered how they were played. Most of the games were made of ivory, and there were also several decks of cards very different from any Nan had ever seen. Not even the numbers on them could be read by the girl because they were in Chinese.

"I wonder if there are any games here I could play with Bert," Nan wondered, her eyes roving about the room.

She did not see any, and in walking to the far end of the room, the girl spied a cabinet which contained a collection of women's tiny slippers. Nan had heard how years before in China girls had had their feet bound tightly to keep them from growing, so she knew these slippers had been worn by women though they were only a child's size. How glad Nan was such a thing had never happened to her!

The Bobbsey girl turned to look at other things in the room. One wall was covered with beautiful tapestries. Each one had a picture woven into it; on one was a dashing horsemen, on another pretty ladies sat drinking tea under a spreading pine tree, and on the third was a gorgeous red and gold pagoda.

"Why, that looks like Sing Foo's pagoda," Nan said, half aloud. "Maybe his building is copied from this picture!"

Some men were sitting on the steps of the pagoda. The door to it was open and inside could be seen a golden dragon.

"I wonder if this means anything," Nan mused, continuing to gaze at the pagoda tapestry. "Maybe it's a clue to one of Sing Foo's secrets!"

She lifted a corner of the beautiful handwork. What she saw behind it made her gasp. Almost unbelieving, Nan reached up and took an object from the wall.

"The Golden Key!" she cried.

CHAPTER XXIII

THE BROKEN STATUE

NAN BOBBSEY dashed from the treasure room and sped through the halls and down the stairway.

"Bert! Flossie! Freddie! Aunt Sallie!" she cried.

When no one answered her, Nan hurried to the kitchen. Mrs. Pry was there, putting a roast into the oven.

"I found it!" Nan shouted at her.

"What's that?" asked Aunt Sallie.

The Bobbsey girl dangled the Golden Key in front of the woman's eyes. Mrs. Pry gazed at it.

"Is that Sing Foo's Golden Key?" she exclaimed. "Where did you find it?"

Nan told her, then asked where the other children were. Upon hearing they all were in the garden, the girl rushed outside. Flossie had just awakened from her nap and was cuddling Smoky in the hammock. Bert and Freddie were weeding a flower-bed.

"Come here quickly!" Nan called to them. "I found the Key!"

Her brothers and sister rushed forward to look at the shiny object in her hand. There was no question as to what it was.

"The Golden Key!" cried Freddie. "Oh, Nan, where was it?"

"In a most wonderful place. Come and I'll show you the room!"

"I'd rather find out what the key fits first," said Bert. "Did you try it any place, Nan?"

The girl admitted she had been too excited to do this. She agreed it would be a good idea to try. She was inclined to think that it would unlock some treasure in the room where it had been hanging. She led the way upstairs.

The other children gasped when they saw the treasure trove. Bert and Freddie wanted to take down the swords at once and look at them, but Aunt Sallie, who had followed the group, forbade them to do this.

"You mustn't touch anything like that," she said firmly. "I'm sure Sing Foo never intended that you children should play with his dangerous weapons."

"I don't see anything in here the Golden Key will unlock," stated Freddie. "It's too big."

This did seem to be true. The various cabinets and drawers which were locked had very small keyholes while the Golden Key was very large.

"Maybe it'll open some secret door behind the furniture," Flossie offered as a solution.

Carefully Bert and Nan lifted each cabinet away from the wall. There was nothing but blank space behind them!

"Perhaps there's a secret trap door in the floor," suggested Aunt Sallie Pry.

Together she and the Bobbsey twins turned up the rug and searched every inch of the place, but they could find no keyhole nor anything resembling a trap door.

"Let's try everything in the whole house," said Flossie suddenly.

"I guess we'll have to," concluded Nan.

First each bedroom was searched, then the group trooped to the first floor. Everything which had a keyhole was tried, but the Golden Key would not fit any of them.

"There's just one place left," said Bert. "The attic! Let's go up there!"

When Aunt Sallie heard what the boy had in mind, she insisted the twins must first eat their lunch, which was ready. The children were so excited and so eager to continue the hunt, they did not want to bother, but Mrs. Pry was insistent.

"There's going to be ice cream for dessert," she said coaxingly.

Since none of the children wanted to miss this, they sat down at the table, but continued to talk about the Golden Key during the entire meal. As soon as they finished the ice cream, the twins dashed to the third floor.

Upon reaching the attic, the children smiled to see the little merry-go-round which the small twins had set up. Freddie wanted to take a ride on it, but the search for something which the Golden Key might fit was more important.

Over trunks and boxes the twins scrambled, trying the keyhole in each one. None was the right size. Once Nan dropped the precious Golden Key, and there were several minutes of panic for the children before they found it. Then they continued the search.

"It's just no use," Nan sighed at last. "The key doesn't fit anything in Mystery Mansion."

Bert was inclined to think maybe Sing Foo had only been teasing them in saying it would unlock a treasure. His twin did not agree.

"Sing Foo is too nice a man to fool us," Nan insisted. "We'll have to figure out what he meant."

The children decided to go downstairs. Just as they reached the second floor, there was a loud crash below. Fearful that something had happened to Aunt Sallie, they sped down the stairs to find out. But the elderly lady was all right. They met her coming from her bedroom.

"Did you just knock, or drop something?" Nan shouted at her.

"No, the clock didn't stop," the deaf woman replied. "What made you think so?"

Quickly Nan repeated her question. Aunt Sallie said she had not knocked anything over and of course she had not heard the crash.

"Maybe Smoky did it," suggested Flossie, and raced to the first floor. "Oh, I hope my kitty didn't break anything."

Bert crowded past his small sister on the stairway and jumped down the steps two at a time. He had noticed that the front door was open. Anything could have happened!

Hurrying to the porch, the lad was just in time to see a boy on a bicycle turning onto the road from the lane which led to Mystery Mansion. He was too far away to be recognized, but Bert had an idea.

"I'll bet that was Danny Rugg," he thought. "Danny has a red bicycle just like the one that boy's riding."

Going back into the house, Bert met the other children. When he told them his suspicion, they wondered why Danny had come back.

"We'll soon find out," said Bert. "I'm sure he was the cause of the crash. Let's look around and see what happened."

At first glance everything seemed to be in order at Mystery Mansion. But upon entering the room where Sing Foo and Bert had put on their shows, the twins gasped in dismay. The statue which bobbed its head had been overturned and now lay in several pieces on the floor!

"Oh, my goodness!" cried Nan.

"What'll we do?" asked Flossie fearfully. "Sing Foo will be mad at us."

Bert was furious. For anyone to come into the house and deliberately break something valuable was the meanest thing he could think of.

"Danny didn't have to go this far," stated the boy angrily.

"You have no proof it was Danny," Nan reminded her twin. "Don't forget that some man has been trying to get us out of this house. Maybe he broke the statue to frighten us."

"You may be right," Bert conceded. "But I'm sure it was the boy on the bicycle."

The children appealed to Aunt Sallie as to what ought to be done about the accident. The poor woman did not know. All she could think of was that she would like to get away from Mystery Mansion as soon as possible. Aunt Sallie did not tell the children this. Instead she said:

"I see nothing to do but pick up the pieces. It will take an expert to mend the statue. I dread having to tell Sing Foo it's broken. After this we must be very careful to keep the doors and windows of the first floor locked."

Bert and Nan felt very bad that they had not helped Aunt Sallie protect Sing Foo's property better than this.

She found a wooden box, and the pieces of the statue were put into it. Nan got a dust pan and broom and the small, broken bits were swept up. Just as the work was finished Flossie, who had made a special trip upstairs, came running into the room.

"I think I know a secret!" she cried out.

The others asked her what it was. The little girl explained she had been upstairs to look at the spot where Nan had found the Golden Key, and was sure she knew what the key would fit.

"It's to the paggody," she said. "That's why Sing Foo put it behind the paggody picture on the wall."

Bert and Nan stared at their little sister. No doubt she had guessed Sing Foo's secret! He had hung the Golden Key back of the pagoda tapestry to indicate that the key would unlock the Chinese building which stood out in his gardens.

"Come on, let's see," cried Bert excitedly. "Where is the Golden Key, Nan?"

The girl still had it in the pocket of her dress. Even Aunt Sallie was so excited she decided to follow the twins. But the woman did not rush from the house the way they did. She stopped to lock both the front and back doors so no one could get inside Mystery Mansion while they were gone.

"Hurry, Aunt Sallie!" Flossie cried.

The little girl ran so fast she tripped and fell. By the time she picked herself up Flossie was some little distance behind the other children. Mrs. Pry caught up with her and together they hurried on. When they reached the pagoda, Nan already had taken the Golden Key from her pocket, and Bert was inserting it in the lock of the door!

CHAPTER XXIV

THE STRANGE MESSAGE

"It fits!" cried Bert Bobbsey excitedly.

Wonderingly he pushed open the large door to the pagoda. It squeaked slightly. The other children and Aunt Sallie crowded in behind him as he stepped inside.

First they could make out little, because it was dark in the pagoda. Nan looked upward. Near the ceiling were several tiny windows. The thought flashed through her mind that this would explain the mysterious lights she and Bert had seen at night. Someone had been inside the building with a light!

"I can't see anything," said Freddie abruptly. "Can't you find a light, Bert?"

"I'll try."

As his eyes became accustomed to the dimness Bert located a switch on the wall. A second later a warm glow of light filled the room.

"Oh!" exclaimed the visitors.

All of them were sure they never had seen anything quite so beautiful before. The walls of the pagoda were of soft red and gold. At the far end was a golden altar with figures of dragons set on either side of it. On the floor lay a silken Oriental rug, and scattered about the room were carved chairs and cabinets of gold.

After the first feeling of awe had worn off, the twins began to inspect the various objects. Aunt Sallie became her practical self once more.

"This place must be worth a fortune," she said. "If I had known about it I never would have offered to take care of Sing Foo's property for him. Too much responsibility."

Nan remarked that it did not look as if anything in the place had been disturbed. She began to think her theory that burglars had been at work in the place might not be true.

"But people have been in here," stated Bert. "We saw lights, and here are some footprints."

Nan stared at the floor. There was no mistaking the marks of dried mud. They had been made by men's heavy shoes!

"Maybe there were small things in here that thieves carried away," said Nan. "Oh, Bert, Sing Foo will be dreadfully upset."

Her twin hardly heard what the girl was saying. He was following the muddy footprints, which led to a heavy door at one side of the room. Something none of the others had seen had caught the boy's eye. He gasped as he looked at it.

"What's the matter?" Nan asked her brother, rushing to his side.

Then she, too, stared in amazement. On the door was tacked a sign. It read:

DANGER
KEEP OUT

"What do you suppose it means?" asked Nan.

"Maybe it's one of Sing Foo's secrets," Bert replied.

Already he had his hand on the knob of the door. His twin pulled him away.

"Please be careful, Bert," she warned him. "The sign says *Keep Out*."

Nan need not have worried. The door was locked, and there was no key in it. She wondered if the Golden Key would fit it, but the hole looked too small. Bert was inclined to think the men who had left the muddy footprints had put up the sign.

"I'll bet they have a lot of Sing Foo's treasures hidden behind this door," the boy said. "Every night they come here and take a few of them away."

"And sell them," Nan added. "Oh, Bert, we should do something about it."

At this moment Aunt Sallie Pry walked across the big room to see what the twins were looking at. Upon reading the sign and seeing the muddy footprints, she became extremely alarmed, insisting that everyone leave the pagoda at once.

"This settles it," she said. "I'm going to telegraph Sing Foo to come home at once. I'm not going to stay here another minute. It's too dangerous."

Bert and Nan pointed out that nothing had happened to any of them. Even if there were burglars around, they had not come into Mystery Mansion, they insisted.

"You're forgetting the broken statue," said Aunt Sallie.

The twins had to admit this, but Bert still felt that Danny Rugg was responsible for the accident. However, he knew Danny could not be held responsible for anything which had happened at the pagoda.

They went outside and carefully locked the big door to the Chinese building. Freddie and Flossie skipped on ahead. They had not understood very clearly what the others were talking about, and were not worried about the *Danger Keep Out* sign.

"I'll race you to the house!" said Freddie to his little sister.

He liked to play this game but his twin didn't, because her brother always won! Nevertheless, she ran alongside of him as fast as she could.

Of course, Freddie reached Mystery Mansion first. He asked Flossie when she caught up to him if she would play outdoors with him.

"What'll we play?" asked Flossie.

"A hunt game."

"What's that?"

"I'll be the hunter," said Freddie, "and you can be any kind of animal you want to."

Flossie giggled. "But you won't shoot me?" she said, already starting to play and pretending to be afraid of the hunter.

Freddie swelled out his chest and thumped it with his fist. Speaking as gruffly and deeply as he could, he replied:

"Hurry, or I'll track you down!"

Flossie was sure the game was going to be a lot of fun. "First I'll be a squirrel," she said. "But you must turn around so you don't see where I go."

Freddie did as he was asked. He counted up to thirty, then looked for his little sister. She was not in sight.

Freddie gazed at the ground where she had been standing. He could see her footprints plainly. Eagerly he followed them, but in a moment they became lost in the grass of the lawn.

"I guess I'm not a very good hunter," the little boy told himself. "Now what'll I do to find the squirrel?"

He looked everywhere but could not see or hear a sign of Flossie. He took so long that she became impatient, and ran from her hiding place in the water lily garden.

"Here I am!" she called out.

Freddie had to admit that his twin had beaten him at the hunt game, and ran down to where she was. Just before he reached her the little girl saw something sticking up in the gravel walk. She leaned over and picked it up.

"A key!" Flossie said aloud.

As Freddie came up she showed it to him. He took it in his hand and then cried out:

"It's the key I found and lost!"

Then Flossie remembered. When the twins had first come to Mystery Mansion the small boy had picked up a key on the road which ran along the side of the property. They had thought perhaps it would unlock the pagoda but before they could try the key there, Freddie had lost it.

"I wonder what this fits," said Flossie. "It isn't as big as the Golden Key."

Freddie excitedly said maybe it would open the door inside the pagoda. He suggested they find Bert and Nan and tell them about it. Flossie thought this was a good idea, but when they went into the house they could find no one there. It did not occur to them to look in the basement where Aunt Sallie and the older twins had gone to see about the big birds which had been fighting that morning.

"Oh, here's the Golden Key!" cried Flossie suddenly, as she spied it lying on the dining room table.

"Let's take it and go try both the keys at the pagoda," urged Freddie.

Flossie was not sure they should do this alone. Freddie argued that since no one was around, what else could they do? So Flossie said all right.

Upon reaching the beautiful Chinese building, Freddie took the Golden Key from his pocket and unlocked the big door. As it swung inward Flossie clung tightly to her brother.

"Oh, Freddie, I'm scared!" she said. "Maybe those bad men are here!"

"They only come at night," said the little boy staunchly.

He found the switch on the wall, and as soon as the place was lighted up they went to the door on which hung the *Danger Keep Out* sign.

From his pocket Freddie took the other key and inserted it in the lock. It turned easily, and he pulled open the door.

The twins had expected to see a room filled with treasures. To their surprise there was nothing but a stairway leading downward. It was totally dark below.

"Let's go back to the house," urged Flossie.

But Freddie would not consider this. He was on an adventure and was going to see it through!

"Here's a light switch," he said, paying no attention to his twin's request.

Freddie snapped the switch and a light gleamed brightly at the foot of the stairs.

"Come on!" he begged.

Flossie really did not want to go; neither did she want Freddie to go. There was no telling what might be down there! Once more she asked her brother to leave, but Freddie would not listen. Already he was halfway down the stairs. Her little heart pounding, Flossie followed him.

Back at Mystery Mansion, Aunt Sallie and the older twins came up from the basement. As they reached the first floor Bert heard the telephone ring and rushed to the front hall to answer it. He was sure the call was from his father, and he was going to tell him the exciting news about the Golden Key. But when he picked up the telephone he was startled to hear a voice say:

"Does Mrs. Sara Pry live here?"

"Yes," Bert replied. He knew Aunt Sallie's right name was Sara.

"I have a telegram for her," said the woman.

"She doesn't hear very well," Bert explained. "May I take the message for her?"

"Have you a pencil?" the woman at the telegraph office asked.

Bert replied that he did, and paper as well. He said he would write down the message as she dictated it to him. His eyes grew wide with excitement as he wrote the words:

SPEEDING BACK BY PLANE. CALL OUT HERE A FAKE. FEAR TROUBLE AT HOME. GUARD EVERYTHING CAREFULLY.

SING FOO

Bert raced to the kitchen to show the message to Aunt Sallie and Nan. But they were not there. He called down the basement stairs and up to the second floor. They did not reply. Finally he went outdoors and saw them near the road which ran past Mystery Mansion. As he hurried toward them, Nan called out:

"Have you seen Flossie and Freddie?"

"No," Bert replied. "I haven't."

"We're dreadfully worried about them," said Nan. "We can't find them anywhere."

The alarming words in Sing Foo's telegram flashed across Bert's mind—"Fear trouble at home."

CHAPTER XXV

THE PAGODA'S SECRET

BERT BOBBSEY told Nan and Mrs. Pry about the telephone message he had just received. At once they too became alarmed over the safety of Freddie and Flossie.

"Oh, I never should have invited you here," said Aunt Sallie fearfully. "Goodness only knows what may have happened to the twins. *Where are they?*"

Nan had an idea. She raced into the house and looked on the dining room table. The Golden Key was gone! Coming outdoors again, she told Bert and Aunt Sallie she believed Freddie and Flossie had gone to the pagoda.

The three hurried through the gardens to the Chinese building. The Golden Key was in the lock. Bert pulled open the door and went in first. The light was on, but Freddie and Flossie were not in sight.

"They're not here!" gasped Nan.

On a hunch, Bert went to the door marked *Danger Keep Out*. A key was in the lock there.

"Come!" he called to the others.

Nan and Mrs. Pry raced to the boy's side. No one spoke, but their hearts were pounding wildly. Were the small twins in trouble beyond the strange door?

When Bert pulled it open, revealing a stairway to the basement, Aunt Sallie insisted upon going down first. But Bert and Nan crowded close beside her. A bright light was on but no one was in sight.

As they descended, the woman put her finger to her lips to indicate the others were not to say a word. They did not know her reason for this, but agreed to obey. Aunt Sallie had begun to think they might find burglars below, and if so, she intended to get herself and the twins out of the place as quickly as possible.

A little corridor at the foot of the stairway had several doors opening from it. Gently Aunt Sallie pushed against the first one. The room beyond was lighted. As she and the twins peered into it they gasped in relief.

"Flossie! Freddie!" cried Nan.

The small children came forward and were amazed to learn they had frightened the others.

"This is a perfectly safe place," stated Freddie. "But it has funny-looking things in it."

"What kind of things?" asked Bert.

"I'll show you," replied his small brother, and led him into an adjoining room.

The older Bobbsey boy gasped. Before his eyes stood a small printing press! Bert knew what it was because he sometimes went into a printer's shop with his father. The others had never seen one of the machines so the Bobbsey boy explained to them what it was.

"A printing press!" said Nan, startled. Then together she and Bert exclaimed:

"The counterfeiters'!"

The small twins did not understand, so they were told perhaps the men who made fake money had hidden their printing press in the basement of Sing Foo's pagoda.

Eagerly Bert and Nan looked around for other evidence. It was not hard to find. Neatly stacked in a box were piles of five-dollar bills!

Bert picked up one and examined the picture of President Lincoln on it. There was no lock of hair on his forehead!

"It's fake money, all right," the boy stated.

When Aunt Sallie realized they were standing in the hide-out of a group of bad men, she became very nervous and insisted they all must leave at once.

"Those dreadful creatures may come back here any minute," she said. "I'm going to get you twins away from Mystery Mansion as soon as I possibly can."

Mrs. Pry put out the lights and hurried the children up the stairway. She locked the door and pocketed the key. Then she hustled them through the pagoda, locked the outer door, and put the Golden Key in her pocket also.

"Oh, I'm glad I got you out of this place," she sighed in relief. "Come, we'll go back to the Mansion at once and pack your clothes."

The twins were sorry to hear this. Freddie and Flossie could see no danger in their staying, and besides, they were having a wonderful time. Bert and Nan were concerned, but they did not want to leave Mystery Mansion right now when things were becoming so exciting.

"Please, Aunt Sallie, don't make us go away," Bert pleaded with her as she hurried the group toward Sing Foo's house. "But I'll call up my father and tell him what we found."

The elderly woman agreed it would be a good idea to call up Mr. Bobbsey at once, but she also thought the twins' father should come out and take his children away.

"I simply will not be responsible for you another minute," she announced flatly.

When Bert telephoned the startling news, his father could hardly believe it. He made the boy repeat his story a second time.

"The counterfeiters' hide-out!" he exclaimed. "I'll get in touch with the police at once."

Bert did not want to tell his father what Aunt Sallie had requested, but to please her he did so. Mr. Bobbsey was inclined to agree that his children should leave the place at once, but he said he would call them back in a few minutes to let them know.

"In the meantime, you had better stay in the house," he advised, and hung up.

While they were waiting for him to call back, Nan and Bert discussed the discovery they had made. The mysterious car; the strange whistles and lights they had heard outdoors at night; the glow which had appeared near the roof of the pagoda;

the threats of the gruff man; all could be explained easily now. The counterfeiters, who must have a key to the pagoda and another one to its basement, came there at night to get some of their fake money.

"Maybe some of them even work there and print more fake money," Nan suggested.

"Yes," said Bert. "And since they couldn't do it with Sing Foo around, they got him to go all the way to San Francisco. But when he arrived there he found it was a trick. You remember the telegram said his call there was a fake."

Nan suddenly had an idea. The counterfeiters knew Sing Foo would come back soon. They would not dare use the pagoda while he was around.

"So they must expect to move out soon," the girl said excitedly. "I hope the police catch the men first!"

At this moment the telephone rang. Bert jumped to answer it. His father was calling to say the police could not thank the Bobbsey twins enough for having given them such a good clue to the counterfeiters.

"They're working out a plan to capture them," Mr. Bobbsey said. "And you children can be of great help to them."

"We can?" exclaimed Bert in surprise.

"Yes, in two ways," his father replied. "You got the license number of the car that stopped near the pagoda, didn't you, Bert?"

"Yes, Dad."

The boy gave his father the number, and Mr. Bobbsey said he was going to repeat it to the police.

There was no doubt but that the car belonged to one of the men who made fake money.

"The police believe the counterfeiters may go out to the pagoda tonight in a truck and remove the printing press," said Mr. Bobbsey. "Chief Smith thinks everything at Mystery Mansion should remain the same so that the men will not become suspicious."

The twins' father went on to say that the children were to stay at the place and play around just as they had done before.

"But you're to stay away from the pagoda," he said. "And you're not to go out of the house after dark."

"All right, Dad," Bert replied. "We'll do just as you say."

"Don't be frightened by anything you may see or hear," his father warned him. "In fact, it would be best if you all go to bed. Nothing will happen to you, because the police will be guarding the house. But, of course, they will be hidden so the counterfeiters can't see them."

After Mr. Bobbsey had finished speaking, Bert told the others what they were to do. Aunt Sallie did not like the arrangement at all and became more and more nervous as time went on. At the usual hour that Flossie and Freddie went to bed they were sent upstairs. Both of them had determined to stay awake and hear the excitement, but they were too weary from the day's adventures and soon fell asleep.

Nan and Bert remained on the first floor with

Aunt Sallie. At nine o'clock they put out the lights and stayed in the kitchen where they could get a good view of the side road and the pagoda.

Nothing happened until eleven o'clock. Then they suddenly saw lights in the distance. A car was coming up the road! As they watched, it stopped near the pagoda and its lights were put out.

"Oh, something's going to happen!" whispered Nan excitedly.

For ten minutes, however, there was not a sound anywhere. Then suddenly the twins heard a shrill whistle. Almost at once flashlights began to appear here and there and the children could hear men running. One bobbed up almost beneath the kitchen window and frightened them.

"They must be policemen!" cried Bert. "Oh, I wish I could go outside and see what's going on."

But the boy would not disobey his father's instructions. Suddenly an automobile drove into the lane leading to Mystery Mansion and a horn tooted loudly.

"It's our car, I'll bet anything!" exclaimed Bert.

He raced from the kitchen, turning on lights as he went. By this time someone was pounding on the front door. When the boy opened it his father and a policeman came inside.

"Did you capture the counterfeiters?" Bert cried.

"Yes, son. They all have been captured."

"Thanks to you, Bert," said the policeman, "and your brother and sisters."

Mr. Bobbsey had expected to take his children

home at once, but when he found that the small twins were asleep he said he would come back in the morning and get them all.

"Dress for school," he suggested, "and I'll take you directly there."

School! Bert and Nan felt as if they had been away from classes for at least a month. They could hardly believe it was only three days. They wondered if ever again they would have so much fun and excitement in such a short time. But they soon were to have them in an adventure called "The Bobbsey Twins at Sugar Maple Hill."

"I wish we could stay here until Sing Foo gets home," said Nan to her father. "There are so many things we have to tell him."

"I'll bring you back some time," he promised, "and by the way, I helped solve another mystery which has been bothering us."

"You did?" said Bert.

"What was it, Dad?" Nan asked.

When the policeman was not listening, he whispered that it was Danny Rugg who had spread the story about Mr. Bobbsey trying to pass counterfeit money.

"And I'll bet he broke the statue here," said Bert. "I'll find out tomorrow."

Bert kept his word. After school the next day he got a confession from the bully. Danny had been so mad, when he had realized that Bert had played a trick on him in the puppet theater, that he had decided to get square. Finding the door to Mystery

Mansion open, he had come inside and broken the statue, hoping the Bobbseys would be blamed for this by Sing Foo.

But Sing Foo was too kind a man to do such a thing. When he returned to Lakeport and learned what Danny had done, he did not even reprove the Bobbsey twins or Mrs. Pry for having left the door unlocked. He told them he had not sold his home and did not mind that they had put a hole in the kitchen wall to rescue their kitten. The Chinese thanked the children over and over again for clearing up the mystery of the pagoda.

"Curiosity of young children often make them find out truth when minds of old men grow sleepy," he said one day when he was having a little party for them at Mystery Mansion.

Smilingly he served fine food, did some more of his magic tricks, and, as they were leaving to go home, presented each of them with a gift. Freddie received a small tank of gold fish. Sing Foo surprised Nan by giving her one of his beautiful white parrots.

Flossie was handed the lovely Chinese baby doll which she had unexpectedly found sitting beside her in a chair at one time. Bert came last, and was delighted to be given a magician's suit which was almost a duplicate of the one Sing Foo wore.

As the other children went to the front porch to get into the Bobbsey car, Bert stayed behind to speak to Sing Foo. He told the man he had found the hidden button which Sing Foo had told him controlled the trick rocking chair.

"I made the chair rock," the boy laughed. "But I didn't tell anyone how it's done. Do you want me to keep it a secret?"

Sing Foo's eyes twinkled.

"Bert," he said, "Sing Foo may need assistant some day. Perhaps you had better keep rocking chair secret of Mystery Mansion to yourself."

THE END

THE END